Michael Underwood and The Murder Room

〉〉〉 This title is part of The Murder Room, our series dedicated to making available out-of-print or hard-to-find titles by classic crime writers.

Crime fiction has always held up a mirror to society. The Victorians were fascinated by sensational murder and the emerging science of detection; now we are obsessed with the forensic detail of violent death. And no other genre has so captivated and enthralled readers.

Vast troves of classic crime writing have for a long time been unavailable to all but the most dedicated frequenters of second-hand bookshops. The advent of digital publishing means that we are now able to bring you the backlists of a huge range of titles by classic and contemporary crime writers, some of which have been out of print for decades.

From the genteel amateur private eyes of the Golden Age and the femmes fatales of pulp fiction, to the morally ambiguous hard-boiled detectives of mid twentieth-century America and their descendants who walk our twenty-first century streets, The Murder Room has it all. **〉〉〉**

The Murder Room
Where Criminal Minds Meet

themurderroom.com

Michael Underwood (1916–1992)

Michael Underwood (the pseudonym of John Michael Evelyn) was born in Worthing, Sussex and educated at Christ Church College, Oxford. He was called to the Bar in 1939 and served in the British army during World War Two. He returned to work in the Department of Public Prosecutions until his retirement in 1976, and wrote almost 50 crime novels informed by his career in the law. His five series characters include Sergeant Nick Atwell and lawyer Rosa Epton, of whom is was said by the *Washington Post* that she 'outdoes Perry Mason'.

Standalone titles

A Crime Apart

Shem's Demise

The Silent Liars

Anything But the Truth

Smooth Justice

Victim of Circumstance

A Clear Case of Suicide

The Hand of Fate

Death on Remand

Michael Underwood

An Orion book

Copyright © Isobel Mackenzie 1956

The right of Michael Underwood to be identified as the author of this
work has been asserted in accordance with the Copyright, Designs and
Patents Act 1988.

This edition published by
The Orion Publishing Group Ltd
Orion House
5 Upper St Martin's Lane
London WC2H 9EA

An Hachette UK company
A CIP catalogue record for this book is available from the British Library

ISBN 978 1 4719 0770 8

www.orionbooks.co.uk

To B. J. H
My godmother

CHAPTER ONE

JULIAN PRENTICE reached prison in three easy stages. On Friday, the fourteenth of March he stole the car. Three days later he pleaded guilty at Wenley Magistrates' Court and three weeks to the day after that he was given nine months' imprisonment by the learned Recorder of Wenley to whose court of Quarter Sessions he had been committed to receive sentence.

Each stage had occupied a minimum of time or fuss and Prentice had been numbed into disbelief by the cruel mischances of fate that had not merely dogged his footsteps but, as it now appeared, had walked hand in hand with him and led the way.

As he sat in the black van rattling back to Wenley Prison, slouched forward and holding his head in his hands, he gloomily reflected that the final stage was over and that only months of dreary, embittering routine lay ahead. If he had cared to think back further he'd have realized that his present plight was but another inevitable milestone in his life's inglorious and downward march. Born of respectable parents and brought up in a decent home, he had stolen from his nurse's handbag at the age of six, forged his father's signature on a cheque at fourteen, been expelled from his eminent public school for theft two years later and first gone to prison when twenty-three. And that was nearly twenty years ago.

He glared savagely at the floor between his feet and let out a contemptuous snort as the gay colours of his old school tie caught his eye. A fat lot of good wearing that had done him. It had definitely turned out to be one of Augustus Jason's less bright bits of advice. The prison van was slowing down and he knew that in a few moments it would pass through the hideously castellated entrance and deposit him without interest on the conveyor-belt of prison life. The van stopped and he heard the driver talking. Then the gate was opened and the van moved forward with a violent jolt so that he was thrown heavily against the side of his mobile cell. He swore softly but soundly, not so much at the driver as at all those who had had a part in the chain of events which had terminated in his present predicament.

'Come on, out you get,' said a brisk but not unfriendly voice.

Prentice got up and, out of habit, carefully brushed the dandruff off his shoulders, though he had no conscious thought of attempting to propitiate the prison reception committee by

1

making himself more presentable. Revenge not propitiation was uppermost in his mind at that moment.

'Come on, you there. Get a move on,' said the voice sharply. He stumbled out into the sunlit yard and gazed with mixed ill-humour and fear at the high wall which now lay between him and life.

Final stage be damned, he thought savagely. Come October and release and they'd soon find out whether all had been for-gotten and forgiven. Till then he must bide his time, even though each minute of every hour would be a reminder. No question here of time being the great healer. He shook himself. Well, at least it was going to be summer and living conditions would be better than had been those at his first boarding school; not that that was saying very much.

So, with a head full of thoughts which bode no one well, he stepped out of the sunlight and into the shadow of the stark building whose monolithic silence gave no hint of the countless teeming and distorted minds it housed.

Augustus Jason, solicitor, strolled back to his office from court, thoughtfully enjoying the genial sunshine. He said 'good afternoon' to a police constable who was standing by the traffic lights in the main street, but was not surprised to receive no answering greeting. In fact the reverse would have been the case since it was an unwritten rule amongst the Wenley Borough Police to ignore him except when duty required otherwise. Jason knew this and felt in no way slighted by the snub; on the contrary rather pleasure that his person was able to arouse such strong feelings in the guardians of the law. He was fortified in the knowledge that it was invariably the police who came off second best in their frequent encounters and that several times when it had been the other way round, they had found their victories to have been distinctly Pyrrhic in the light of after-events.

Slowly he climbed the narrow staircase which led to the cool and dingy offices which his firm occupied. He stopped before the glazed door which bore the inscription 'AUGUSTUS JASON & CO., Solicitors and Commissioners for Oaths' and tilted his battered, grease-stained hat on to the back of his head. The stairs were becoming a nuisance in that they were a constant reminder that he was not getting any younger. Though he had been in practice on his own in Wenley for some thirty-five years, he was only just sixty; and sixty, he quickly reminded himself, wasn't old by present-day standards. And now Claudia had qualified and joined him, and a dream had come true.

Walking past the deserted inquiry desk, he stopped for a moment outside his daughter's office, his fingers resting lightly on the door-handle. Then he quietly went in. Claudia Jason, of whom it had been said that she was as popular and attractive as her father was the reverse, was staring out of the window with her thoughts a thousand miles away. She started as the door shut with a click.

'Sorry if I made you jump, Sweetie,' Jason said.

'I didn't expect you back so soon', she replied, as if she'd been caught in some guilty act. 'How did it go? The usual bind over?'

'Alas for Julian, no. Nine months.'

'Good gracious,' Claudia said in a not displeased voice, 'what went wrong?'

'I can't imagine. It was the fifth case in the list. The first four got the standard avuncular scolding. You know the theme: this way lies perdition and destruction, etc., but because I believe there's some good in you, I'm going to give you another chance; I'm going to bind you over to be of good behaviour, etc.'

'The silly old fool's voice absolutely throbbed with mawkish sentiment as four villains followed each other into the dock. The various expressions of contrition they put on were so spurious that no one other than our own learned Recorder could possibly have been taken in by them.'

'Well, thank heaven, Prentice didn't get away with it too,' Claudia said firmly and went on, 'quite honestly, I'm delighted that he's gone to prison. That's where he deserves to be.'

'Tut, my dear, that's no way to speak of a cherished client.'

'Cherished client, my foot. He's nothing but a plausible rogue and we've got too many such clients. Clients, indeed', she added disdainfully.

'I've never pretended to have a so-called high-class practice but, by heaven, it's a prosperous one', her father said with a touch of acerbity in his tone. 'People don't have to show me their family trees before I'll take them on as clients. All I'm interested in is their money.'

'Yes, nasty, greasy pound notes with an elastic band round them', she replied in a tone of disgust.

For a moment Augustus Jason studied his daughter thoughtfully. The quality of his practice was always a potential source of friction between them. Claudia had only recently qualified as a solicitor and he supposed it was natural that she should still be filled with starry-eyed idealism about the ethics and integrity of their profession. Furthermore, having served her articles with another firm, she had had no intimate knowledge of her father's practice until she had arrived just under a year ago as his junior partner – the first partner that he'd had in thirty-five years.

This, however, was by no means the first time that she had registered her disapproval of the class of practice which for so long he had conducted with great success and profit and which

3

had made him a host of implacable enemies, not least the Wenley police from whose grasp he frequently managed to rescue slippery wrongdoers. The fact was that their difference in professional outlook was profound. He interpreted the solicitors' code of ethics with extreme elasticity and, provided there was sufficient reward in terms of hard cash, was not averse to conduct which most members of the profession, including his daughter, would not countenance and which, if discovered, would certainly give the Disciplinary Committee of the Law Society something to think about.

Nature's gifts had combined with experience to make him an able lawyer and a hard man. But like many hard men, he had an Achilles heel. In his case it was Claudia. She alone was able to evoke in him the tenderer human sentiments; all his other relationships being governed by expediency.

He smiled at her and gently stroked his ragged moustache which was stained yellow in the centre and often, it seemed, in danger of being set alight by the fractional cigarette end that peeped eternally from between his lips. His rheumy and rather repelling eyes softened behind the veil of cigarette smoke which drifted upwards.

'Don't let's quarrel about it, Sweetie. One day you'll realize perhaps that just as it takes all sorts to make a world, so must there be solicitors to cater for every class of client, including the Julian Prentices and other small-time crooks of this life.'

Claudia turned away and looked out of the window. Then suddenly she switched round and faced her father again, her cheeks glowing with all the beauty of a ripe peach.

'But why did you have to appear for Prentice on this of all occasions? Don't you realize how awful it looked? He's charged with stealing my car and you defend him.'

'But, Sweetie, you know I wouldn't have dreamt of representing him if a plea of guilty hadn't been inevitable from the very outset. There was never any possibility of my having to cross-examine you or question your evidence. And anyway what did the latter amount to? Simply that you'd left your car outside the office here, unlocked and with the ignition key in, and that Prentice had no authority to take it.' He paused and added, 'It was incontestable on any view of the case.'

'Maybe, but it was your doing that he pleaded not guilty to stealing but guilty only to the minor charge', she said, refusing to withdraw her accusation. The charge to which she referred and to which Prentice had pleaded guilty was one of taking and driving away a car without the owner's consent contrary to Section 28 of the Road Traffic Act 1930.

'But, of course, he never stole the car. There wasn't the slightest evidence of any intent permanently to deprive you of

4

its ownership. It was a pure case of joy-riding. On the other hand he had no answer to the Road Traffic Act charge.' He didn't add 'and more's the pity' though this was how he felt about all his court cases which resulted in pleas of guilty and thereby deprived him of one of his favourite pursuits, namely attacking police evidence.

Claudia looked primly severe and said, 'I should have thought that there was a clear inference to support the stealing charge, but there's no point in our arguing about it any further. All I repeat is that I'm very glad he's been sent to prison and that in the circumstances I don't think you showed great taste in defending him, even if he is a *cherished client*.' Then foolishly she added, 'Particularly as he's done it before: taken someone's car without their permission, I mean.'

'But no charge was ever preferred against him on that occasion', Jason said quickly.

'Presumably only because he had too much of a hold over Tom Notley', she retorted.

He eyed her with cool appraisal and then said quietly, 'Don't forget that one of the first requirements of our trade is discretion and a careful tongue.'

Tossing her head crossly at the rebuke to which she had exposed herself and showing exaggerated interest in the papers on her desk she said:

'If you'll now excuse me, I must get on with that Leadbetter conveyance.'

A few moments later her father left her office and Claudia sighed heavily. She was genuinely fond of him and loyal to him too, though heaven knew how difficult that was at times when the whole of Wenley knew him as 'The Shady Solicitor'.

'Paper?'

Stanley Irwin Potts, J.P., Borough Councillor and late Major R.A.S.C., held out the *Wenley Evening Post* to his wife, Eileen, who was turning the pages of the *Parish Magazine* without interest as he came into the room.

'I think you'll find it better than what you've got there', he went on as he sat down in his chair before which was placed his customary tray of tea. Nursing the enormous mug which he always used, he watched her intently as she glanced at the front page.

It was exactly a quarter to six, the hour at which he was wont to arrive home with the precision of clockwork and the scene was a routine one in their lives. Routine, however, only on the surface for recent months had seen their lives inexorably transformed until it was this element of routine which alone gave them any semblance of normality and held things precariously together.

'You'll see that Prentice got nine months', he said after a long pause.

Eileen stiffened and fiddled nervously with her spectacles.

'Oh, did he?' She managed to make her tone sound casual.

'It's about a quarter of what he deserved. Anyone other than our Recorder would have given him a proper sentence.'

'I don't know why your Justices didn't deal with the case themselves in the first place, seeing that you're all always so dissatisfied with the Recorder's sentences.'

'Because, quite rightly, they didn't consider their powers of punishment sufficient.'

'Rather ironical then that they might have given him more than the Recorder', Eileen said in a deliberately irritating tone.

'That's where you're wrong', her husband said smugly. 'Six months was the Statutory maximum a Magistrates' Court could have inflicted in the case.' He had recently been appointed deputy Chairman of the Wenley Borough Justices and took his judicial duties very seriously and always enjoyed trotting out small tit-bits of legal knowledge. 'The fellow has been a pest in this town for too long and it's high time he was put behind bars for a substantial period.'

'Anyone would think you had a personal vendetta against him the way you carry on', Eileen said, and immediately regretted having spoken.

'He's an associate of Notley's. Isn't that sufficient?' Potts said fiercely. She looked away and the colour mounted in her cheeks. 'Well, isn't it?' he persisted.

'Surely we needn't go into that all over again?' she said evenly.

'No? Not even when it's a case of one's wife carrying on with a garage proprietor for all the town to see. Why, only two days ago at a council meeting. . . .'

'Stop picking a quarrel', she broke in sharply. 'I won't sit here and be talked at like that. One day you'll say one word too many and. . . .'

'Oh, so now you're starting to allocate the blame in advance. . . .'

'Stanley, I'm telling you . . .' she said quietly but in a tone full of meaning. She got up and for a few moments they stared at each other in silence: he baleful and she warning against further recrimination. She was tall and thin and her bespectacled school-mistressish face was mild and impassive as she looked at her husband who sat forward on the edge of his chair as if preparing for a leap across the room. She still had the evening paper in her hand and carefully folded it before speaking again.

'Have you a meeting tonight?' she asked.

He nodded curtly. 'The General Purposes Sub-Committee.'

There was scarcely an evening when he didn't have a meeting and there never had been a more assiduous committee member in the whole of Wenley. If he managed to get adopted as a parliamentary candidate, which was his current ambition, someone would have to put more than seven days into a week for him.

Eileen sighed and turned towards the door. As she walked across the room she could feel his eyes burning into her back and trying to read her thoughts. She was half-way through the door, when he spoke.

'I'm sorry, darling. Truly sorry that I spoke as I did just now.' He shrugged his shoulders in a gesture of helplessness. 'I know how mean of me it was: how much I have to be grateful to you for.' At this point he waved a vague hand round the comfortably furnished room and continued, 'I promise I'll try and keep my side of the bargain in future.'

Eileen's expression plainly conveyed her intention of reserving judgment on the good faith of his protestation. She gave him a faintly quizzical smile and a moment later had left the room.

Councillor Potts, or Major Irwin Potts as he preferred to be known, thoughtfully nibbled the top of his thumb and frowned heavily at the patterned Aubusson carpet.

Tom Notley viciously crumpled the *Wenley Evening Post* into an untidy ball and hurled it into a corner of his tiny office. Next he removed his feet from the desk, reached for the telephone and dialled a number. As he did so he leant back and slammed the door, not so much to exclude the hideous noises from the workshop which reverberated round the whole garage as to ensure that his conversation would not be overheard.

Small though his office was, it had cost him a lot of money to have it made sound-, fire- and burglar-proof; most garage offices being the reverse of these things.

While he waited for the phone to be answered, he doodled busily on his blotter and several times shook the receiver impatiently. When at last a languid female voice came down the line, he spoke briskly.

'Oh you've decided to answer at last, have you? I want to speak to Mr. Jason . . . Mr. Notley. . . .' There followed a series of clicks and whirrings and then Augustus Jason came on the line. 'Where the hell have you been, Gus? I've been trying to get you this last hour. Anyway, what the hell went wrong? I thought you told me he was certain to be bound over or whatever you call it.'

'I thought he was, but for once the Recorder broke form and sent someone to prison.'

'Too bad it had to be our Julian, if you know what I mean. Was he very sore about it?'

'He was certainly a bit stunned and may, I suspect, feel a little sore when he comes round', replied Jason dryly.

'I'm not surprised. I suppose I shall have to see what I can do for him. It wasn't by any chance a case of your not having your heart in the job, Gus? It being your daughter's car and all that?'

'That's a most unworthy suggestion. You know I always do my best for my clients.'

'Mmm', Notley said non-committally. 'When does he get out?'

'In six months' time if he earns full remission.'

'I suppose that bastard Potts put a spoke in his wheel.'

'I don't follow you', said Jason with a note of caution in his voice.

'Nobbled the Recorder I mean. Probably the beaks would have dealt with it if he hadn't got at them too. Did he give evidence to-day?'

'Since Julian pleaded guilty, no one apart from the police has given evidence at any stage. I explained that to you the other day.'

'Maybe you did, but I wouldn't put it past that so and so to get in an extra jab if given half a chance.'

Augustus Jason pondered this in silence for a moment or two and then said gently, 'It was bad luck his being recognized by Potts and only because he had to brake to avoid those Boy Scouts.'

'Yes, wasn't it?' retorted Notley, elaborating his doodle with a sudden flourish. 'Did his previous convictions come out?'

'Of course they did. It was on account of them that the Justices considered their powers inadequate and sent him forward for sentence.'

'I don't see that they were so bad. His previous convictions, I mean.'

'No, they weren't. Just a few minor peculations.'

'Plus that one for peddling dirty books.'

'Yes, there was also that', agreed Jason easily.

'Maybe the Recorder didn't like the colours of his old school tie,' said Notley unkindly and then quickly continued before Jason had time to offer any comment, 'O.K., Gus. It's a pity but I gather there's nothing more to be done. At any rate I must think about it. By the way I want to come round and see you tomorrow about something else. O.K.?'

It appeared that it was and their conversation finished. Notley got up from his chair, deftly opened the wall safe and tossed a small pocket diary into the back of it. Then he carefully relocked it and stepped out of his office into the main part of NOTLEY'S GARAGE (WENLEY) LTD.

8

Thirty miles away in a neighbouring county, Dominic Trevane, an amiable young man in his mid-twenties, sat flopped in a chair with one leg swinging over the arm.

Being a pleasantly ordinary person ungifted with any psychic or prescient powers his eye did no more than skim casually over the paragraph describing Julian Prentice's appearance that day at Wenley Borough Quarter Sessions. He yawned contentedly and quickly turned to more interesting news on the sports page.

Later he didn't even recall having read the account. Not that it made any difference to events either way.

CHAPTER TWO

SIX months later on a golden October morning, Julian Prentice stood once more in the prison yard; this time on the verge of release. The various stages of discharge had been completed except for the final one, the opening of the main gate and the short step across its threshold to freedom.

His personal property had been returned to him and in addition he had been given a small sum of money and a large amount of well-meant advice. He had accepted the one and rejected the other with an equal display of impassivity.

'Be good.' The cheery admonition came from a prison officer on his way off duty and was accompanied by a sly wink. Prentice eyed him with disfavour and heard him mutter 'sour bastard' as he disappeared round the corner of one of the prefabricated buildings in the yard.

A few minutes later all formalities had been completed and he stood outside the gate which was re-barred with such haste that he wondered whether his immediate attempt to re-enter had been expected.

A hundred yards down the road to his left was a stationary car parked just where the letter had said it would be. Even at this distance he could see that it was empty and awaiting him. He walked slowly toward it. There didn't seem to be any need to hurry and it gave him more time to ponder the day's programme; not that he had done much else during the past few months.

A callow, spotty youth materalized at his side from nowhere.

'You Julian Prentice?' he asked breathlessly. 'I'm the Press.'

'Well push off', Prentice said curtly. The youth took a step back in temporary alarm as he found himself the object of a

9

thoroughly malevolent stare. 'Go on, get on your bike and pedal back to your editor.'

With a safer distance between them, the youth mustered his dignity and said, 'There's no need to be like that. I only. . . .'

'Scram.' The word had never before been made to sound so mandatory and this time the youth complied.

Prentice stood and watched him cycle off down the road and only moved when he had disappeared out of sight. He reached the car and walked round it with feline interest. It was a four-door saloon of a popular make and by its appearance not very old.

He opened the door and got into the driving seat. The ignition key was in position and the engine came to life at the first press of the starter. He let it run for a few moments before engaging a gear and slowly moving off from the kerbside.

Hardly was he under way when there was a klaxon blast behind and he felt drops of cold sweat trickle down his spine. So it was a trap after all, flashed through his mind. Before, however, he had time to think further, an ancient truck laden with crates of vegetables hurtled past on its way into the town and with its passing all became silent again.

Shaken, he stopped the car and looked about him. Though there wasn't a vehicle or soul in sight, it was some time before his confidence was restored and he was satisfied that no sleek police car lay lurking in wait for him.

By the time he reached the left-hand turn half a mile down the road he had quite regained his nerve and was revelling in the feel of driving a car again.

A few yards before the turning he slowed down and changed gear and then lightly flicked over the indicator switch. Immediately there was a shattering elemental roar in his ears and his conscious world dissolved into a series of blinding coloured flashes, followed by waves of black enveloping darkness.

CHAPTER THREE

BLAST, as everyone with a recollection of the war years will know, is full of tricks and is quite unpredictable in its effects. Thus, when by all rights Julian Prentice should have been blown to small bits or at the very least rendered limbless by his experience, he was merely bruised, lacerated and severely shaken.

That the explosion brought good to no one, least of all, of course, Prentice and the car, is furthermore not true, since the spotty youth was not only a witness to the incredible event but the sole witness thereto, and so found himself spoon-fed a scoop of unimagined proportions.

One of those, however, to whom the matter was distinctly irksome and unwanted was Detective-Inspector Playford, head of the Wenley Borough Police C.I.D. He was a large, placid man who disliked being hurried and who deplored any intrusion of official business into his home life. On the morning of Prentice's near removal from earth the telephone rang at a quarter to nine just as he was finishing his breakfast in ruminative silence.

'It's for you', his wife said, sticking her head round the kitchen door. 'It's the duty sergeant. He's all excited. Something or other's happened.'

'What?' he asked with a sinking feeling.

'I didn't ask him. It's you he wants to talk to.'

Inspector Playford sighed heavily and went into the hall to hear the worst. He listened in silence with growing dismay as Sergeant Sweet retailed the known facts in a few succinct sentences.

'All right, I'll be along right away', he said gloomily at the end and replaced the receiver. It really was too bad. Only a month to go before his retirement, an event toward which he had for some time been coasting effortlessly, and now this. It sounded all too much like hard work and it was with a heavy heart that he bade his wife good-bye, fitted himself into his small car and drove down to police headquarters.

'The Chief wants to see you', said Sergeant Sweet rather too brightly as he went past the desk.

'He here already?'

'Came along as soon as I phoned him.'

'You never told me that you'd phoned him', Playford said reproachfully.

'Didn't I? Sorry: but I thought you'd know anyway. Routine on a job like this one.' Sergeant Sweet spoke in an airy tone. He could afford to. He was an up and coming young officer who had favourably caught the Chief's eye. Not so Inspector Playford.

Slowly he made his way upstairs to the Chief Constable's office on the first floor. It was a large and light room in the extremely well-appointed building which had been completed a few months before the outbreak of war in 1939.

'Come in', the Chief Constable called out briskly as he knocked on the door. Then, 'Ah, here you are. I was just about to get them to give you another ring.' He didn't wait for any apology, explanation or protest but continued, 'You've heard what's happened, of course?'

11

'I gather a man has been injured in a car explosion, sir', Playford said stolidly.

'Not just a man', replied the Chief tartly. 'It's that fellow Prentice who got nine months for stealing Miss Jason's car.'

Inspector Playford did some laborious mental arithmetic and said:

'I didn't know he was out yet, sir.'

'He was released at eight o'clock this morning', the Chief replied with a touch of impatience. 'I've been through to the Governor and this must have happened within twenty minutes or so of his leaving the prison.'

Playford nodded sagely and reflected with melancholy that a Detective-Inspector was almost superfluous when a force had a Chief Constable who tried to do everyone's job in addition to his own. This wasn't, of course, true, but the new Chief, who had held the appointment for only a year, was an energetic man and held the view that the head of his C.I.D. invariably needed a red-hot poker to galvanize him into action. Part of the trouble lay in the fact that he was fifteen years younger than Playford and had taken up his new appointment after a short lifetime of brisk and efficient service with the Metropolitan Police Force in which he had held the rank of Superintendent (uniform branch) immediately prior to his translation to Wenley. It had taken him but a few days to decide that several of the senior members of his new force needed pepping up and this he attempted to achieve by a combined tactic of leading, tugging and prodding all at the same time. Or as the officers concerned would have it, 'by bloody interfering'.

'I've sent Detective-Sergeant Whiteside to the scene to find out what he can about the car and you'll have to go along to the hospital and see Prentice.'

'How badly hurt is he, sir?'

'I've spoken on the phone to the doctor who examined him', said the Chief with the smug air of one well aware of his efficiency. Happily at the same time he was quite unaware of his Detective-Inspector's own treasonable thoughts. 'He's pretty badly shaken up but I gather there's no reason why he shouldn't be able to give you a statement.'

Inspector Playford's last hope vanished. He had banked on Prentice lying in a convenient and obliging coma for several days while he orientated himself and set about persuading the Chief that it was a case for outside help.

'Amazing thing is he wasn't killed', the Chief continued. 'Certainly no fault of the person who fixed the device in the car that he's not a murderer instead of only being an attempted one.'

Inspector Playford thoughtfully sucked his lower lip.

'I suppose there's no hint as to who that person is, sir?' he asked forlornly.

'None yet; though I hope it won't prove beyond your resources to find out.' The Chief Constable paused for a moment and went on, 'Revenge, paying-off an old score, ensuring silence; any of those may provide the motive. The man's got a criminal record and a careful scrutiny of his past will almost certainly be fruitful.'

'Yes, I expect so, sir', replied Playford without enthusiasm. 'If, however, sir, I don't get an early lead, you may consider it a case for calling in the Yard. It's a bit out of the usual run. Exploding cars I mean, sir.'

The Chief Constable fixed him with a steely look.

'Your suggestion is premature, Inspector, and does not, I'm afraid, reflect a very healthy or confident outlook on your part. There'll be time enough to consider the point when I know whether you've been able to make any headway with the investigation. Well, I won't detain you further. Report to me later in the morning when you've been to the hospital and seen Prentice.'

Inspector Playford was on his way out of the room when the telephone rang and the Chief Constable put up a hand to stay him.

After emitting a series of staccato monosyllables, he put down the receiver and said:

'That was Sergeant Whiteside. He has found out that the car came from Notley's Garage. It was one of their hire ones.'

Playford knew most of the staff at the Wenley District Hospital. In a town the size of Wenley which had a population of between sixty and seventy thousand, it was part of the job of the police to know all the leading personalities, besides a great many others possibly less leading but no less useful.

It was just after ten o'clock when he arrived at the hospital and was greeted with friendly waves and nods from members of the staff as they hurried to and fro. They were a sincere testimony to his popularity and if there appeared to be any lack of deference to his position it was only because of the impossibility of according such to anyone whose fallen arches had once been the life and joy of the Orthopaedic Department.

A small white-coated doctor bustled forward. He was one of the casualty officers and Playford knew him well. His name was Dr. Czakowski.

'Hello, Dr. Jack', Playford greeted him.

'You would like to see this man, eh, Inspector?' Dr. Czakowski asked in his carefully articulated English.

'Is he fit enough?'

'Yes, but you must not stop too long with him and you must not excite him, otherwise. . . .' The doctor left the word to speak for itself. He assumed a mock lugubrious air and raised eyebrows, shoulders and the palms of his hands in a gentle gesture designed to express his inability to foretell the imponderable future.

'But he's conscious?'

'Yes, he is conscious and he is able to talk and also to understand what is said to him, *but* what effect this how-do-you-call-it may have had on his mind. . . .' He tapped his head dramatically and finished the sentence with another gesture.

'What exactly are his injuries?' Playford asked.

'I will tell you', Dr. Czakowski replied with the air of one about to reveal life's great enigma. 'He has had much skin removed from his left and his right buttocks and he has many small foreign bodies embedded in his flesh in that part of him. It is there that he received the full force of the bang.' He spoke with relish and went on to describe in detail other injuries of a more intimate nature to this portion of Julian Prentice's anatomy. Finally he said, 'In addition he is somewhat deaf from the . . . from the . . . what is that word? Not bang, I know.'

'Explosion.'

'I thank you, yes, from the explosion and is mildly shocked.'

'All things considered he seems to have got off very lightly.'

'It will need surgery to remove all the tiny fragments of foreign matter from his backside; but I agree that he is lucky.'

'To be alive.'

'Of course, yes. No one is lucky to have a skinless behind.'

'Well, I'd better see him, Dr. Jack.'

'O.K. I will take you to him.'

Dr. Czakowski led the way to where Julian Prentice lay screened off at one end of a small public ward and left Inspector Playford at the bedside.

'Remember you must not excite him', he admonished as he turned to go.

Prentice fixed Playford with his one unbandaged eye but said nothing. He was propped and slung at an angle which made him appear like some beached and battered boat, and his hands which lay outside the bed-covers were both heavily bandaged.

Playford decided on a hearty approach.

'Well, Prentice, they tell me you're not too badly hurt and will soon be up and about again.' While he spoke Prentice kept an unwavering eye on him, but looked away as soon as he stopped. He said nothing.

'Do you feel up to answering a few questions?' Still there was no response and Playford went on, 'You appreciate, of course, that we've got to find out what happened to you and who did it?' He paused waiting for an answer but still the man in the bed remained silent, though it was apparent that this was by choice and not as a result of any injury. In legal jargon, mute of malice and not by visitation of God. 'Look here, Prentice, this attitude won't do you any good. You'd much best answer my questions.' Then in a more cajoling tone, he added, 'Don't you want whoever it was to get booked for this?'

'What do *you* think, Inspector?' The words were quietly spoken and were accompanied by another cyclopic stare.

'That's more like it', said Playford jovially. 'Now the first thing is, have you any idea who might have tried to blow you up?'

Prentice appeared to ponder the question seriously. After a considerable pause he said, 'No.'

Playford frowned. Clearly the man was stalling. He must have some ideas on the subject.

'Were you expecting a car to meet you at the prison?' he asked patiently.

'Yes.'

'A car without a driver that is?'

'Just so.'

'Who was sending it for you?'

'A friend.' He managed to divest the word of any agreeable connotation.

'By the name of?' asked Playford coaxingly.

'That you must find out some other way, Inspector.'

'Where were you driving to when it blew up?'

'Quite frankly I don't think I'd made up my mind which was to be my first port of call.'

Playford sighed but determined to persevere.

'It was one of Tom Notley's cars, wasn't it?'

The eye was turned on him again and Prentice said evenly:

'Why ask if you already know?'

'It looks like it may have been he who tried to fuse you?' Playford went on.

'If you say so, Inspector.'

'It's got something to do with your last conviction, hasn't it? The time last March when you stole Miss Jason's car?'

'All these highly leading questions, Inspector', said Prentice in a tone designed to exasperate. 'And you must be more careful what you say. Nobody *stole* her car. Somebody may have taken and driven it away without her consent; but stole, never.'

'O.K., Prentice, be clever if you want to, but don't think that this stubbornness will do you any good. Furthermore let me say this. So far as I am concerned, it's the greatest pity

15

that whoever it was bungled the job of blowing you out of this world. If he'd succeeded it would still have meant a good deal of work for me but there would have been the compensation of knowing that you were finally and for ever out of my hair, you mean little crook.'

He glared at the recumbent figure.

'You're much more attractive in your true colours, Inspector', Prentice sneered. 'But don't despair, I may yet decide to enlist your aid.'

Inspector Playford decided on his parting shot. In an almost pitying tone he said:

'You don't for one moment imagine, do you, that the chap who tried to kill you will rest until he's completed the job? If at first you don't succeed, try, try, try again and you can bet your bruised hide that's precisely what he'll do. So if I don't see you again till you're on a mortuary slab, make the most of the next few days.' He turned swiftly on his heel and stumped out while Prentice watched him with an expression of mingled scorn and fear.

Playford stood on the steps outside the hospital and lit his pipe. When it was going well, he squared his shoulders and sniffed with appreciation the delights of a mellow autumn morning. It was obvious that a visit to Tom Notley was next on the agenda and that it mustn't long be delayed. Furthermore it would be an interview which would have to be handled in just the right way if it was to be in any degree successful.

He had known Notley since he came to Wenley in 1946 and set up in business as a garage proprietor. By dint of hard work, considerable business acumen and a fair measure of ruthlessness, he was now the owner of a flourishing concern which in the last few years had made him one of the town's wealthy citizens. He was unmarried and lived in a flat which was furnished with the maximum of luxury and minimum of tastes and where he had the reputation of spending leisure hour, in endless seduction.

Playford respected him but trusted him no more than he would a grizzly bear; both, in his view, being deceptively friendly to the casual observer. No one seemed to know much about his antecedents and it was generally suspected that his origins were humble and that with his rise in the world he had cut adrift from all family ties. He was wont to speak about his service in the 1939–45 War when he attained the rank of Warrant Officer in the Royal Engineers. Ten years later he was one of Wenley's most prosperous residents with a finger or suspected finger in many pies, large and small; also in others of unspecified size and flavour.

16

Slowly Playford walked down the steps. By the time he reached his car he had decided to go and see Notley at once and to call in at police headquarters on the way; not to render any homage to the Chief Constable but to find out whether Detective-Sergeant Whiteside had yet returned from his end of the inquiry and, if so, with what results.

As he drove into the yard at the back of headquarters he saw a large group of officers gathered in interest round something which for the moment lay out of his view. A moment later he could see that it was the car. It had just been towed in and Sergeant Whiteside was standing beside it like a salesman who, for once, has something really worth-while to show off. Playford couldn't help reflecting that it was fortunate that the Chief Constable's office faced the other way. He pushed his way through the throng.

'Well, here she is, sir', Sergeant Whiteside greeted him cheerfully.

Playford had no love of things mechanical and regarded cars merely as useful means of getting from A to B. He stared at the car without affection. To him, it had now lost its purpose in life and was only fit to be consigned to a scrapheap.

'What have you found out, Norman?' he asked, gingerly touching with a fingertip the driver's door which hung precariously on a single hinge.

'It's all right, sir, we've been over her for fingerprints. Did that before we towed her in. Neat job: the left indicator was disconnected and the switch on the steering-wheel had been rewired to the charge which was obviously placed beneath the driver's seat.'

'You mean,' Playford said carefully, 'that the charge was exploded when Prentice went to put out the left indicator?'

'That's how I reckon it was done, sir. Mr. Jameson from the laboratory is on his way over to make a full examination but I don't expect him to find out anything different', Sergeant Whiteside said complacently.

'You're one of these amateur radio johnnies: how expert would you have to be to fix a device like that?'

'Oh, not very difficult, sir. Anyone with an elementary knowledge of electrical circuits or radio could have done it quite easily.'

'What about an ordinary motor mechanic? Could he also have fixed it without any bother?'

Sergeant Whiteside nodded without hesitation and said:

'I reckon so, sir. As I've said, it was a perfectly straightforward job for anyone with a bit of expert knowledge.'

'I see', Playford said gloomily; each new fact persuading him further of the difficulties of solving the case. 'What about the explosive? Dynamite?'

17

'Hardly', said Sergeant Whiteside with a patronizing laugh. 'Much more likely to have been gelignite or gun-cotton.'

'Why are you so positive about that?' Playford asked, somewhat nettled by his subordinate's tone.

Sergeant Whiteside was taken aback. He knew very little more about explosives than his inspector but hadn't expected to be cross-examined on the subject quite so sharply.

'Dynamite's a different thing altogether', he said airily. 'Used for blasting rocks and that sort of thing. Seems much more likely that this was the type of charge that's normally used for blowing up tree stumps and that sort of thing', he concluded hazily.

'Such as gelignite and gun-cotton?'

Whiteside nodded in hearty agreement and at the same time let out an imperceptible sigh of relief that he had bluffed his way through.

'Or – that sort of thing', Playford suddenly added with great sweetness.

He peered without enthusiasm into the interior of the car and Sergeant Whiteside, anxious to redeem himself, said:

'You'll see, sir, that the main force of the explosion seems to have been in the direction of the back of the car. If it had been upwards through the seat, I doubt whether Master Prentice would now be alive.'

'More's the pity', murmured Playford. He turned away from the car. 'I'm going out now. I'll be at Notley's Garage if I'm wanted. You'd better hang on here till Mr. Jameson arrives.'

Notley's Garage (Wenley) Ltd., was situated on the London road on the southern fringe of the town. It was a fine new structure with white-coated petrol-pump attendants, a showroom full of miraculously new-looking second-hand cars and other trappings necessary to attract the choosey customer.

Playford parked at the side of the garage and made his way to Notley's private office which led off the back of the showroom where it was divided from the workshop. The door was half open and he could see Tom Notley bent forward over his desk. He must have heard Playford's footsteps since he looked round suddenly and said:

'Ah, here you are at last, Herbert. Come on in. Hey! mind out!' As usual Playford had forgotten the step down and arrived in the tiny office as if out of a catapult sling. Notley pulled out a chair from the corner for his visitor and swivelled himself round in his desk one to face him. 'Tch, just look at your trousers', he said as he sat down. Inspector Playford peered ruefully at the fresh oily stain on his right trouser leg and Notley went on, 'We'd better do something about that now. I'll get a drop of petrol.'

He disappeared outside the door and returned a moment later. Playford watched him nonplussed as he worked away at the stain with a piece of rag soaked in petrol.

'There, that's done it, I think, Herbert', he said as he straightened up. He tossed the rag through the door, closed it and sat down.

Inspector Playford felt discomfited. The tiny incident had somehow managed to put him on the wrong foot and he almost wondered whether it had not been deliberately devised by Notley to embarrass him. Though he realized that the thought was ridiculous, Notley's own air of complete assurance did nothing to allay his malaise.

For a time the two men looked at each other in silence. Then Notley said:

'Well, Herbert, go on.'

'How do you mean?'

'I take it you're paying me an official call in connection with the destruction of one of my hire cars. Right?'

'Yes, that's what I've come about, Tom.'

'O.K., fire away then.'

But still Inspector Playford seemed to find difficulty in launching his questions. If he had been disposed to indulge in a little quiet self-analysis, he would have realized that his difficulty arose from Notley's confident air of having a full supply of ready answers to anything he might ask.

'You admit it was one of your cars, do you?'

'Don't be daft, Herbert, of course it was one of mine.'

'And how did it get outside Wenley prison this morning?'

'I presume it was left there by the young chap who hired it', Notley replied easily.

'Who was that?'

Tom Notley spun his chair round, picked up a piece of paper off his desk and spun back again.

'His name,' he said, 'was Richard Dyson and his address is forty-six Sussex Terrace, Wenley. It's one of those roads the other side of the goods station', he added helpfully.

'I know it', Playford replied. 'Prentice had lodgings there at one time.'

He thoughtfully examined the piece of paper which Notley passed him and said:

'Perhaps you'd better tell me all you know, Tom.'

'Sure I will. That's just what I want to do. Are you going to take it down in writing or what?'

'No, just tell me your story and we can reduce it to writing later.'

The sentence tripped automatically from his tongue. In police circles statements are never written but always reduced to writing. It was, however, the first part of it that seemed to cause Notley some concern.

'I don't like the use of that word "story", Herbert. I remember Gus Jason once telling me that some judges always talk about the case for the prosecution and the story for the defence. A subtle but unattractive distinction, eh?'

'Let's have the facts, anyway', Playford said placatingly.

'Well, it was about five minutes past six yesterday evening. All the staff had left and I was about to lock up and go when this young fellow arrived. At the time I thought he was a bit het-up but didn't pay much attention to it. He said his own car had broken down and he desperately needed one to get to some dance or other and that he'd bring it back this morning. I got the impression from him that the whole party would fall through unless he could get hold of a car. Normally I would have said "no" to someone coming along at such short notice, but ... well he seemed a decent chap and was ready to pay a substantial deposit in cash – yes, in cash', he repeated, catching Playford's eye. 'And what's more I'm afraid the money was paid into the bank first thing this morning before I knew anything about what had happened. As I was saying, there was a car available and everything seemed to be in order so I let him have it. That's really all there is to it.'

'A bit of a rush job?'

'It seemed so at the time, though looking back now it was obviously all part of a plan.'

'Would you be able to recognize this chap again?'

'Certainly I would.'

'Describe him.'

'He was somewhere in the mid-twenties; had fairish hair; medium height.'

'Sounds a fairly common type of young man.'

Notley shot him a quick glance. 'He was, but are you being sarcastic, because if....'

'Don't take offence so easily', Playford interrupted in a soothing tone. 'What else did you notice about him?'

'He was wearing a blue blazer and a pair of grey flannels', Notley said sullenly.

'Notice the colour of his eyes?'

'Does one man ever notice the colour of another's eyes?' Notley replied in a scornful tone.

'Yes, sometimes. Anyway, what else about him? Was he clean shaven?'

'Yes.'

'Have you got a specimen of his writing?'

Once more Notley spun round to his desk and then back again to hand Playford a book.

'I imagine you'll want to take this away with you. There's the entry in my writing,' he said pointing, 'and there's his signature.'

Playford took the book from him.

'I take it you'd never seen him before?'

'No, never. As you may know, I have a pretty good memory for faces but his was definitely new to me.'

'And there was no one else on the premises when he called?'

'No, dammit, there wasn't. I know what you're thinking but I can assure you that *I* had no reason to try and kill Prentice.'

'But it's a bit awkward for you, isn't it?'

Notley stared at him with hostility and Playford went on, 'Were you in touch with Prentice while he was in prison?'

'I went to see him once and I also wrote to him once.'

'Recently?'

'No, soon after he got there.'

'He used to work for you here, didn't he?'

'You know quite well he did.'

'But he wasn't at the time of his last conviction?'

'No, he wasn't: and stop your insinuating.'

Playford stood up. By putting out a hand, he could, if he'd tried, have touched all four walls from where he was standing.

'Must be a cosy little office in winter', he said conversationally. 'By the way, can you think of anyone who might want to implicate you in this job?' To point the finger of suspicion, as the song goes?'

'No, certainly not', Notley said quickly.

Playford nodded as though he hadn't expected any different answer. He stepped through the door, turned back and said:

'Incidentally, I've warned Prentice that I fully expect the chap to have another shot at killing him. I reckon he's in greater danger now than he was before.'

Notley's eyes narrowed.

'Yes?' he said, passing a hand through his thick mop of curly black hair, 'but why are you telling *me* this?'

'Just thought you might be interested: you're a friend of his.' He moved as if to go, then turned back a second time and said pleasantly, 'I don't think I mentioned it, but there's no such address as forty-six Sussex Terrace. But you probably know that anyway.'

CHAPTER FOUR

THE next morning Augustus Jason arrived early at his office. He had scarcely hung up his hat and looked quickly through the pile of letters on his desk when he was aware of voices in the corridor outside. One, that of his secretary, was mildly demurring: the other, which he immediately recognized, was distinctly peremptory in tone. Meanwhile both were getting nearer to his door. A moment later it opened and Miss Strang, his secretary, stood there looking hot, embarrassed and ashamedly aware of her failure to hold a visitor at bay.

'It's Major Irwin Potts', she said. 'I've told him I didn't know if it was convenient but. . . .' At this point, Potts's face appeared over her shoulder.

'I had to call and see you, Jason', he broke in. 'I'm on my way to court, so I won't take up much of your time; but it's important.'

When he had finished speaking, he and Miss Strang both looked at Augustus Jason as if for adjudication. Since Miss Strang was managing to fill the doorway with her solid presence, Potts was unable to enter without recourse to physical measures and these, though perhaps contemplated, were happily not taken.

'Seeing that you've taken the office by storm, you'd better come in', Jason said with a shade of annoyance. At this cue Miss Strang stood disdainfully aside as if to let the plague past, and Potts brushed quickly by her as she turned to retire to the hinter regions of the building.

'Well, what's the trouble?' Jason asked as soon as they were alone.

'Who said anything about trouble?' said Potts sharply. 'I just wanted to see you about this affair yesterday.'

'Prentice's near demise, you mean?'

'Yes. The point is that I don't want to be dragged into it in any way.'

Jason peered at his visitor through half-closed eyes and a drifting cloud of cigarette smoke.

'But why should you be?' he asked.

'Isn't it clear that it's somehow connected with his recent sojourn in prison?'

'Mmm.'

'Well, I was concerned with the case that led to his being sent there.'

'I follow you', said Jason slowly, having in fact understood all along. 'You think the police may start delving into the past?'

'I'm quite sure they will and don't forget I was a witness against him; or would have been, at least, if he hadn't pleaded guilty.'

'But even if the police do come and see you, what can you tell them except that you were a witness of his accident in

my daughter's car last March and' – he went on with a malicious
glint in his eye – 'that you had the indignity of sitting down
heavily in a puddle when he swerved to avoid a troop of Boy
Scouts.' He paused and then added, 'Isn't that the sum total of
your knowledge of the matter?'

Potts didn't reply immediately but appeared to study Jason
closely for a time. Then he said:

'You're not usually obtuse, you know – unless you mean to
be and then you usually confine it to your appearances in
court.' He took a deep breath and continued, 'Isn't it crystal-
clear that Notley's responsible for the attempt on Prentice's
life? Don't ask me why he did it; though I imagine that he and
Prentice each knows more about the other than is really safe for
either. It can only be a matter of hours before he's arrested and
charged. Anyone other than that old stick Playford would
probably have pulled him in already. Now do you see what I mean?'

'Your wife and Notley?'

Potts's mouth hardened and he gave a grim little nod. Even
then he still managed to look boyish and Jason, wondering
why, decided that it was on account of his hair. It fell across
his forehead in a schoolboy fringe, and an irregular and not
very well defined parting terminated at the crown in a thicket-
like tuft. It was grey-flecked at the temples and this together
with the two unmistakable lines round his mouth alone gave
some indication that he might be over forty.

Jason half-whistled to himself as he appeared to ponder the
position. Finally he said:

'But isn't it fairly common knowledge about your wife and
Tom Notley?' Potts looked uncomprehending and he explained.
'What I mean is, that the scandal (it that is the right word) is so
widely known in the town that surely no further harm can be
done to you by their names being linked together.'

'It's bad enough having one's wife's name mentioned in the
same breath with that of a garage man, but it's infinitely worse
when he turns out to be a near murderer', Potts said querulously.

Augustus Jason pursed his lips and wished he could be certain
of the real reason for the visit. Surely the man must realize that
there was nothing he could do to prevent people talking. Though
Potts wasn't particularly popular in local public life, often dis-
playing a fine range of obstinacy both as a J.P. on the Bench
and as a councillor in municipal debate, there had been no
attempt by anyone to make capital out of his unfortunate
domestic affairs and Jason couldn't see that Notley's arrest
would affect him. Furthermore, rumour had it that the association
between Eileen Potts and Tom Notley was finished and Jason
certainly had his own reasons for believing rumour to be truthful
on this occasion.

23

'In any event your wife and Notley have not seen so much of each other recently, I believe?'

'Eileen has finished with him. That's why it would be so damnable to be involved in this affair.'

Jason sat silent for a moment. Then, shrugging his shoulders a trifle impatiently, he said:

'I'm sorry, but there doesn't seem to be much I can do for you, Major Potts.' He refrained from expressing any of the caustic comments that came to his mind, having long since learnt the value of keeping his thoughts to himself; and on this occasion he was certainly not without them.

Somewhat to his surprise, Potts made no effort to prolong the interview but got up and walked to the door.

'No?' he said. 'Well, for a start you can replenish your stock of libel and slander writs. In the second place (and I hope you won't take this amiss) I would like you to think twice before agreeing to represent Notley on his arrest.' He looked at Jason, his head cocked slightly on one side and added, 'And as to that, if they don't pull him in soon, I have no doubt he'll complete the job he bungled yesterday – and that won't be a bad thing for society.'

He departed leaving Jason to stare fixedly at the door for several minutes apparently lost in deep thought. The manner of his arrival had portended so much more than had in fact transpired and Jason pondered on where and why the interview had changed its course.

He was still pondering when the office inter-communication set on his desk buzzed and Miss Strang announced that Mrs. Irwin Potts had just arrived and would like to see him urgently.

He had no time to reflect on the significance of a second unheralded visit by a Potts before she was shown into his room.

'It's very good of you to see me at such short notice,' she said breathlessly as she sat down, 'but I had to come and consult you about it.'

'It?' asked Jason in mild surprise.

'Yesterday's business over that man Prentice and the car. What do you think will happen now?' As she spoke, her eyes searched his face anxiously.

He stared back at her appraisingly. Her usual calm and placid expression had become an ill-fitting mask and above all her eyes betrayed a state of unnatural anxiety.

'What will happen?' he echoed softly. 'The police will investigate of course and if they find sufficient evidence to prefer a criminal charge against anyone, they'll do so, one supposes.'

'Is it quite certain that someone will be charged with attempted murder?'

Jason looked at her with curiosity.

'I don't know', he said. 'The police are not given to taking me into their confidence.' After a pause, he added, 'May one ask why you're so interested in the matter, Mrs. Potts?'

Eileen turned her head away from him and spoke in a whisper.

'Because of Tom Notley. I can't bear to think of his being arrested and locked away in prison.' She looked back at him suddenly and with imploring eyes continued, 'You will do everything you can for him – for us – won't you?'

If he was surprised, Jason didn't show it.

'My dear Mrs. Potts, you really shouldn't anticipate events in this way; especially since they may never happen.'

'May never happen', she repeated thoughtfully. 'That's it, isn't there something you can do now to forestall them, something so that the police never do arrest him? I know what a clever lawyer you are, Mr. Jason.'

Jason studied her covertly. He was considerably more puzzled by this visit than he had been by that of her husband. Something didn't fit at all.

'I take it your husband knows nothing of your coming to see me', he said after a brief silence.

'Oh, no! He left early to go to court and I came along as soon as I'd done the chores.'

'I see. Well, I don't think there's any need for you to worry at the moment. When you come to your hurdles, then will be time enough to decide how to jump them. Sometimes one can even avoid jumping them at all', he added with a small and not very attractive chuckle.

Eileen didn't appear to be reassured and in a sudden rush of words said:

'But supposing, despite everything, Tom Notley is arrested, how much will come out?'

'That depends on many things. On what the police know, on what they can prove, on what they want to prove – and also on what they can find out.' He emphasized the last words and staring her out of countenance said in a quietly insinuating tone, 'That's what is really worrying you, isn't it, Mrs. Potts? You're afraid they may find out something about you and Notley which, shall we say, could have somewhat unfortunate consequences? Something your husband doesn't yet know about, for instance?'

She nodded and, plucking nervously at the strap of her handbag, said softly:

'Yes, something like that.'

'Well, I wouldn't worry: it may never happen.'

She looked at him with an air of resignation, then suddenly held out her hand and smiled.

'Thank you so much, Mr. Jason. I'm afraid I've taken up your time with a lot of silly female nonsense. I think I must have temporarily lost my sense of perspective.'

'Please don't apologize. It's always a delight to see you.'

'How is your daughter?' she asked conversationally as she moved toward the door.

'She's well.'

'You must be very proud having her with you in the office.'

Jason smiled mechanically but his mind was clearly elsewhere as he opened the door and ushered her out. It was with considerable difficulty that he turned it to the pressing problem of advising his next client how to skate nimbly round a fettering clause in his lease.

Meanwhile in her office at the other end of the corridor, Claudia Jason also had a visitor; though whether he could strictly be called a client was debatable. It certainly was not the pursuit of legal advice that brought him to the offices of Augustus Jason & Co. on this particular morning.

Dominic Trevane sat frowning on the edge of her desk, swinging one leg.

'Don't look so worried', Claudia said lightly.

'Does it show that much?'

'Yes, and it did last night as well. Has anything happened?'

His wide mouth broke into a grin which somehow only managed to underline his uneasiness.

'Nothing, darling. It's just . . . just that I don't like the idea of your going out with this man Notley.'

'Oh, not that again!' she exclaimed with exasperation born of the slightly censorious note which he was unable to keep out of his voice.

'I don't like the broad passes he keeps making at you', he said stolidly. 'He's not to be trusted.'

'Oh, do lay off, Dominic. I'm fully capable of looking after myself, I promise you that. I'd never have told you about him last night if I'd thought you would make so much fuss.'

'But it's only natural I should dislike the thought of your going out with him.'

'Don't think about it then,' Claudia exclaimed crossly and went on, 'whatever next! Since when have I been your personal and private possession? And what's more I've known Tom Notley a whole lot longer than I have you. He's been one of the firm's clients for years, whereas you first came to the office only a month or so ago.'

Dominic looked momentarily sheepish.

'Time has got nothing to do with these things,' he said with an upsurge of confidence, 'and you've got to admit that you like me much better than him.'

'Don't be so sure about that. Tom Notley has a great deal of charm.'

'The sort that every sugar daddy has', he replied in a tone which was half flippant and half serious. 'He's old enough to be your father.'

'That's a silly remark,' Claudia said and added severely, 'look, I've got a full day's work to do, so now you'd better go.'

'Not before you promise to meet me this evening.'

'I've already said I will.'

'And never to see Notley again.'

'I've already told you I'm going out with him tomorrow night', she said and looked him challengingly in the eyes.

'We'll see about that later', he replied grimly, but then leant quickly forward and lightly kissed the tip of her nose. Before she could protest, he gazed at her in mock alarm and said, 'I do believe one of the freckles has come off.' He pretended to remove it from the tip of his tongue and to try and stick it back on again, but this time Claudia took avoiding action.

'You really must go, Dominic, or I shall never get through my work. I shall start charging you for use of my official time.'

'To one kiss on the tip of the nose and removal therefrom of one freckle, say five guineas.' He darted forward again but Claudia, anticipating the manoeuvre, backed away.

'No, Dominic,' she said firmly.

He sighed resignedly and heaved himself off the desk.

'When we're married, you. . . .'

'No one has yet said a single word about marriage', Claudia broke in hastily. 'Now go away or I shan't keep our date tonight.'

Dominic's brow clouded:

'O.K., but don't forget you're not seeing Notley tomorrow. You'd better ring him up and tell him.'

Before Claudia could join issue with him over this, the door opened and her father came in.

'Oh, it's you, Trevane, is it?' he said eyeing Dominic who stood awkwardly by the desk. 'You're not in trouble again, I hope.'

Dominic blushed.

'I just dropped in to see Claudia on a private matter,' he said and then feeling that some further explanation was required of him, added, 'I had to come over to Wenley on business this morning.'

Jason gave him a studiously polite smile which he found as disconcerting as it was intended to be. Turning to his daughter Jason said:

'Well, my dear, if you and Mr. Trevane have finished your *unofficial* business, perhaps I might have a word with you on an *official* matter.'

27

At that moment the phone rang and Claudia lifted the receiver.

'It's for you', she said handing it to her father.

'Hello', he said. 'Yes, put him through.' Placing his hand over the mouthpiece he hissed, 'It's Notley.'

Dominic who had been hovering in a state of apparent indecision hurriedly muttered, 'I'll be off', and was gone. Jason gave his daughter a quizzical lift of the eyebrows which she chose to ignore and then Notley's brisk and forthright tones came down the line. They were clearly audible to Claudia as she busied herself over at a filing cabinet.

'Look here, Gus, I've got to see you. Things are getting uncomfortable and I don't propose to sit back and do nothing. You know what I mean of course.'

'Yes, I know what you mean', replied Jason.

'Well then, I'd like to come round this morning.' There was a pause and he added, 'Hello, are you still there?'

'By all means come round, Tom, but I don't promise to accept your instructions.'

'What the hell are you talking about?'

'It might be a good thing if you found yourself another lawyer.'

'But I don't want another. I'm quite satisfied with you.'

Jason smiled sourly and said:

'It's a pity I can't reciprocate the sentiment.'

There was silence for several seconds and then Notley spoke again.

'I'm coming over to see you straight away and if there's any more of this nonsense I'm going to be bloody annoyed. Now's the time I particularly want my solicitor's help and now's the time I mean to have it, Gus, so stop trying to shove me in the dog-house.' As an afterthought he added, 'If you think you can frighten me away from your daughter by taking this line, you've got another think coming.' In a less angry tone he continued, 'Someone is obviously trying to frame me over this Prentice business and we've got to do something about it quick or they'll have me inside. So don't you try and shop me now, Augustus Jason. I'll be over in about twenty minutes.'

'And I'll be waiting for you', Jason replied. There was a vague hint of menace in the words, accentuated by the theatrical air of finality with which he dropped the telephone receiver back on its rest and stalked from his daughter's room.

The morning was slowly drawing to a close and all in court save *one* were conscious that the hand of the clock had passed five minutes to one and that pangs of hunger were beginning to

demonstrate themselves in small individual exhibitions of impatience. The *one* was Mr. Mutton, a local solicitor with an immensely ponderous manner and a complete disregard for time.

Major Irwin Potts, flanked by Miss Montague-Burphitt and Mr. Coke, respectively an ex-Indian Army General's daughter and an engine-driver, sat like a posed group depicting ennui through the ages while Mr. Mutton, delighting in every cliché known to a hack advocate, went on and on. His client who was charged only with driving gently across a set of traffic lights after they had turned red was as bored as anyone in court. If he had known it was going to be like this, he would have gladly pleaded guilty some two hours before. But now the issue was irrevocably joined and an air of fatalism hung all around them.

At last Mr. Mutton reached his peroration. It was a heady brew consisting of several mixed metaphors, two Latin legal tags and a rare but abundant helping of misquoted evidence and irrelevant law.

As he sat down, flushed with exertion, Potts and his two fellow justices came slowly to life. There was no need for them to consult together. A quick look at each of them, two nods and Potts was able to say:

'We find the case proved.'

'Nothing known', said the court inspector without pause or wasted word.

Assuming his most judicial expression, Potts swelled, with much more facility than Aesop's frog, into Major Irwin Potts, J.P., and pronounced sentence.

'There'll be a fine of ten shillings.'

As the words fell from his lips, the door at the back of the court burst open and Augustus Jason hurried forward to the solicitors' seats.

Mr. Quench, the Clerk to the Justices, was at that moment standing on his chair talking to Potts and consequently had his back to the rest of the Court. When he turned round and saw Jason, his face assumed an expression of disagreeable surprise. It had been a trying morning and it was only by concentrating his mind on his wife's specially prepared Irish stew that he'd got through the last half-hour at all.

'The Court has adjourned, Mr. Jason', he said testily.

'Indeed it has not. Their Worships are still here and I have an application to make', retorted Jason.

'An application?' echoed Mr. Quench in heavy sarcasm. 'Surely you know they must be made at ten-thirty before other court work begins. You can't possibly make an application now.'

'I can and will. There's no law restricting the time when

29

they have to be made. Just because it's your practice to hear them first thing doesn't preclude their Worships from doing so at any hour of the day or night.'

'This is intolerable', said Mr. Quench, who, in addition to everyone else, cordially disliked Jason. 'I won't have my court upset like this. Look at the time, it's nearly ten past one.'

'And it'll soon be a quarter past if you don't let me get on with my application. Furthermore it is not *your* court – fortunately.' Elevating his gaze to Potts who sat blinking uncertainly on the Bench, Jason said, 'May it please your Worships, I wish to make an application for a summons. . . .'

'Who are you appearing for?' Mr. Quench broke in sharply. 'Perhaps you'll at least have the courtesy to tell us that.'

Jason ignored him.

'I'm making this application on my own behalf. . . .'

'Your *own* behalf?' spluttered Mr. Quench.

'If your learned clerk can hold his peace for two consecutive seconds, I can make my application quite shortly and in language which I think even he will be able to follow.'

There was silence. Jason had won the first round and now waited a moment so that the fact could sink in.

'My application, your Worships, is for a summons for assault against one Thomas Notley.' Ignoring the buzz of excited whispers that immediately broke out in every part of the court, he went on, 'He attended at my office this morning and when I refused to take his instructions in a certain matter he lost his temper and struck me in the face with his fist.' At this point he indicated just beneath his left eye where the skin was slightly red.

Meanwhile Mr. Quench decided that it was time to re-assert himself.

'Come, Mr. Jason,' he said in his most deliberately offensive tone, 'surely you're not asking the Court to issue a summons on such flimsy material.' He fluttered an expressive hand indicating just how flimsy some material could be and continued, 'Isn't that one of the occupational hazards of a solicitor in your type of practice? I really couldn't advise their Worships to issue process simply on what you've just told us – *even* if they should accept every word you've said.'

What might have happened next must remain in the realm of speculation for as the two men stood silently drawing fresh strength for the next round, Detective-Inspector Playford burst into court and, unaware that he was interrupting any business, hurried up to one of his subordinate C.I.D. officers.

'Come back with me to headquarters straight away', he said urgently. 'Prentice has vanished. He's walked clean out of the hospital and we've *got* to find him before it's too late.'

The two officers dashed out; but not before Playford had

noticed the very strange effect this startling news had on both Jason and Potts.

CHAPTER FIVE

TWENTY-FOUR hours later, Prentice was still missing. He had vanished as completely as a raindrop in the ocean.

At twenty minutes past twelve the previous day he had been lying in bed with the blankets pulled up to his neck (it was now obvious that this had been to conceal that he had got surreptitiously dressed): ten minutes later when a nurse had brought him his lunch, she had found the bed empty. It was a small ground-floor ward and the open window told its tale. The only other occupant had been wheeled back from the operating theatre but half an hour before and was still under an anaesthetic. Thus to all intents and purposes, Prentice had been alone.

What puzzled Detective-Inspector Playford was the completeness of the disappearance. It was without trace and though Prentice must have been seen before he found refuge, no one had come forward to say so.

From the police point of view the problem of finding him was furthermore complicated by the fact that he was not an escaped or escaping felon; on the contrary he was a victim of felony past and in all likelihood of further felony to come. This had an inhibiting effect on the search for him and necessitated an irksome by-your-leave approach. It was always much easier to hunt the felon himself since altogether ruder and more efficacious tactics could then be employed.

All this passed through Playford's mind as he sat despondently in his office and mopped his brow. It had been a long and tiring day and still he saw no prospect of getting home to supper at any reasonable hour. On the other hand the Chief Constable had a few minutes before phoned from home to make some brisk suggestions and Playford had almost been able to sniff the saddle of mutton and red-currant jelly off which he had just been dining.

Detective-Sergeant Whiteside came into the office and flopped uninvited into a chair.

'He's just melted away, sir. Someone must be hiding him in an attic or a cellar.'

'Or in a bath of acid', Playford said seriously.

'You think he may be already dead, sir?'

'I should say there's a very good chance of it.' Showing unwonted emotion he went on, 'Blast this modern fashion of vanishing victims in murder cases. Why the blazes do they have to give us all the extra trouble of looking for the body? Soon we'll have murderers sitting grinning on our doorstep while we lark around playing hunt the corpse.' He made an expressive sucking noise with his teeth and continued, 'Well, you'd better get out on the search again. I'm not leaving here tonight till every bit of waste-land, every, well, every murky nook and cranny in this town has been scoured.'

'And if we do find his body, sir?'

'We'll have a certain gentleman inside these four walls even quicker than it takes you to down a pint of beer.'

At about the same time that Sergeant Whiteside was sallying forth from police headquarters, Eileen Potts was dumping the supper things in the kitchen sink where they would await the attention of Mrs. Merlin, their daily woman, the next morning.

Coming downstairs a few minutes later, she put her head round her husband's study door. His pipe was going well and he sat in his large armchair, the floor around him littered with documents. There were the minutes of the last council meeting, a batch of pamphlets which had arrived only that morning from party headquarters in London and a memorandum by Mr. Quench on some recent High Court decisions circulated with the twofold design of keeping the Wenley Justices up to the mark and showing them what an admirable clerk they had.

'I'm just off', Eileen said in a flat tone.

'Have a good meeting, dear', her husband replied without looking up. 'Shall I expect you back the usual time?'

'I suppose so. Nothing you want before I go?'

'No thank you, dear', he said with an abstracted air as he picked up a pamphlet enigmatically entitled 'The Dollar Gap and YOUR BREAKFAST'. Eileen was about to close the door when he turned his head and added, 'Are you expecting any phone calls this evening?' She shook her head and he said with a short laugh, 'Fine, though I don't doubt there'll be some.'

As she walked down the drive, she drew her coat tightly around her, though it was a far from cold evening. Out on the pavement, she looked nervously up and down the road. It was quite deserted. Then moving with unexpected speed and hugging the inside of the pavement against the garden walls, she hurried off in the opposite direction to her meeting. At the road junction four houses along she paused and again looked all around her. Then with a final swift movement she was round the corner and in the public telephone-box which stood twenty yards down an unmade-up and badly-lit road. It was an infrequently used call-box and nobody really knew why it had been erected there. But to Eileen it was a haven.

She inserted three coins and dialled a local number. As she waited for an answer which, it soon became apparent, was not forthcoming, her expression became increasingly agitated. Eventually she replaced the receiver, having first regained her coins, and then with an air of desperation picked it up again and dialled another number. This time the distant brr-brr alone broke the stillness of the atmosphere. It went relentlessly on till at last she dropped the receiver back on its rest and, without bothering to reclaim her pennies, pushed her way blindly out of the box and melted into the darkness.

Tom Notley and Claudia had dined well, though for Claudia it had not been a pleasurable meal and she would have willingly forgone the excellent food and accompanying wine if her father and Dominic had not by their autocratic conduct forced her into keeping the date. She comforted herself with the thought that to have given in to either of them by breaking it would have been as fatal as Samson agreeing to be shorn of his hair. No, she reflected, it was infinitely preferable to have eaten the food, drunk the wine and endured Tom Notley's increasingly inebriated company.

She drained her coffee-cup and sat back aware of Notley's eyes roaming greedily over her face and body. The wine waiter approached and placed a small thistle glass of bénédictine before her and a large balloon one of brandy before Notley.

She met Notley's eyes and said:

'But I said I didn't want a liqueur.'

'It's good for you', he replied with a lecherous grin. 'Helps to settle the stomach after dinner.'

'But my stomach is perfectly all right – though it probably won't be if I drink this.'

His grin widened.

'You must drink it now it's come.'

Claudia decided not to make an issue of the matter, confident that both her stomach and her head could safely stand the extra alcoholic load. She lifted the glass and took a sip.

Notley watched her approvingly and slowly poured a large measure of brandy into his mouth where he held it a while before swallowing. She really was a very desirable young girl and he wondered in rosy fuddledness why he hadn't been aware of her charms long before. How that old rogue Augustus Jason ever came to sire such a daughter was yet another genetic mystery. He reckoned that if he could induce her to return to his flat for a nightcap, the rest should be easy. The difficulty, he correctly foresaw, was going to be in persuading her to come to the flat; though to this end the glass of bénédictine might prove a useful ally.

33

He himself didn't often get drunk and he wasn't really so now. He had simply achieved that happy state when certain of the senses are comfortably dulled and libidos become aroused like torpid giants waking from their sleep. For the moment his cares had assumed their proper place in the background and ceased to hold the stage, and he was blissfully unmindful of anything but the immediate present.

'I hope you're glad you came out with me this evening', he said, suppressing a mild belch.

Claudia smiled doubtfully.

'So far', she said lightly.

'That's good. I must say you're a very remarkable girl.'

'I suppose I now have to ask you in what way?'

'Coming out with me like this after my row with your father.' She shrugged her shoulders and he went on, 'You've obviously got a mind of your own.'

'A girl needs to have these days.'

'But they haven't all got them. Mind you, I don't think strong-willed girls make the best wives,' he prattled on, 'though then of course it's up to their husbands to tame them.'

Claudia made no reply but composed her features into an expression of polite and detached interest. She reflected how glad she would be when the evening was over and there was no further necessity for her to go out with him again: that is provided Dominic and her father didn't try and dictate to her. Not that her father had had any opportunity of doing so on this occasion since she had carefully refrained from telling him with whom she was dining, thereby showing that prudence was another of her qualities.

'A girl without a will is like a cocktail without gin. Very insipid', Notley continued, savouring his smile with obvious pleasure. 'Mind you, a girl like yourself has got to be careful not to carry your professional manner into your social life. Nothing is more certain to frighten a man off than a woman with a cold, businesslike manner.'

If Claudia had thought that this or any other sort of manner would frighten off Tom Notley she would have been more than glad to give it a try. It was clear, however, that he was too set on executing his plan to capture the castle for anything now short of commando shock tactics to deter him.

She looked ostentatiously at her watch.

'I really think . . .' she began.

He nodded with a hopeful gleam in his eye.

'I'll get the bill', he said. While they were waiting for his change to be brought, he went on, 'I don't think you've ever seen my flat, have you?' Claudia shook her head as she might have done in refusing a second cup of tea. 'I think you'll like it.

I've got some new curtains in the living-room which you must give me your views on. I think they're very pretty and I don't mind telling you they were b. expensive. Not that one minds paying when one knows one's getting value. And these are good value. You see I happen to know the chief salesman of a firm which. . . .'

By the time he had finished his account of how he'd acquired such splendid curtains at such a bargain price, they were on the pavement outside the hotel.

'I say, something wrong?' he suddenly asked, putting an arm round her waist.

Claudia moved away from the questing arm but it was clear from her momentarily distracted manner and the twin spots of colour on her cheeks that something had happened.

'No, nothing, thank you', she said quietly.

'I thought maybe you'd seen a ghost.'

'No, it wasn't a ghost', she replied in a coldly even tone.

'Well, let's get back to the flat and have a drink.'

'If you don't mind . . . I must be getting home.'

'But of course I mind. I mind very much. I want you to see my new curtains.'

'I'd love to another time.'

'No, tonight. I insist', he said with drunken truculence.

'Now, don't go and spoil a very pleasant evening by bullying me', she replied, trying to mollify him with a smile.

'But the evening hasn't begun yet.'

'For me it has *and* ended', she said with a light laugh. 'Don't forget I'm a working girl.'

But Notley was not to be so easily placated. He looked at her with angry eyes trying to make up his mind on the next move. He was breathing heavily as the last double brandy began to step up his blood pressure. Claudia pretended that she hadn't noticed anything untoward about his behaviour, though she anxiously longed for the impasse to be quickly and painlessly resolved.

Suddenly he grabbed her arm tightly and started to force her along the pavement.

'Come on,' he said thickly, 'you'll enjoy yourself when you get there.'

With an upsurge of anger and fright she said, 'Let go of my arm and don't be so silly.'

She tried to struggle free but the grip was unrelenting and she found herself being propelled along to where his car was parked. If she were to scream, help would undoubtedly be forthcoming, but in the circumstances a scream must be the last resort. Once released, its repercussions could be endless. She dug her heels into the pavement.

'Let go at once', she said fiercely.

'This is the only way to treat strong-willed girls and really they love it', he said with a nasty laugh.

Claudia realized that she was only one move off the irrevocable scream. Swinging her whole body round, with her free hand she slapped his face with all her might. There was a resounding smack and instinctively he released his grip of her arm and shot a hand up to his stinging cheek. As soon as he let go of her, Claudia ran.

When finally she stopped for breath, she was a good two hundred yards down the road from the hotel. She slackened her pace and walked on, gradually becoming more composed, and in due course found herself outside his garage. She noticed that his car was parked at the side of the building and concluded that he must at some stage have passed her on the road. She stared at the dark façade. Just past his car, the small high window of frosted glass which she knew to be that of his office shone a dull yellow and a faint glimmer of light also showed beneath the side door beyond it.

By now anger rather than fear had taken charge of her emotions and as she stood fuming on the opposite pavement, she was seriously minded to go across and follow up her physical assault upon him by a verbal castigation.

A moment later the side door opened and then very quickly closed again.

It was about a quarter of an hour after this that a passer-by noticed a strange flickering glow coming from the frosted office window. Even as he looked again, the glass shattered and a licking tongue of yellow flame slithered through, followed by a curl of black smoke.

Another seven minutes went by and the Wenley Fire Brigade arrived at the garage and assumed control. It was not a difficult fire for an experienced crew since the blaze was confined to Tom Notley's own tiny office, where the specially constructed fire-proof walls had shown their worth by preventing the outbreak from spreading to the more inflammable parts of the building. Indeed they had performed their allotted task, though in a cruelly perverse fashion.

The firemen found the door to the office locked on the outside; but the key was in the lock. When they threw it open, it was like looking into a blast furnace and the outward surge of heat sent them reeling back.

It was several minutes before they could safely enter the by then sodden and acrid atmosphere. A body lay grotesquely humped on the floor, horribly charred and beyond normal recognition.

CHAPTER SIX

'HAVE a pickled onion. It's the new jar', Mrs. Playford said to her husband.

Though his plate was already piled high, he dived his fork in and speared a couple of the small succulent onions, lodging them precariously on the mound of food which was now almost ready for his assault. Then with slow deliberation he spread a slice of bread with just sufficient butter to cover its surface. It was an operation which absorbed all his attention and his wife watched him with a worried expression.

'Forget about Prentice and enjoy your supper, dear', she said.

'I'm going to', he replied. 'What's more, I don't mind what the Chief Constable thinks.'

Each of them knew this to be untrue, and it both troubled and annoyed Mrs. Playford that a man as conscientious as her husband was such an easy prey to a harrying Chief Constable.

'You're not going back to the office again this evening, I hope.'

Inspector Playford shook his head.

'Not unless anything happens. The whole inquiry is completely gummed up. We haven't found Prentice and without him we can't get anywhere – whatever the Chief may say and think', he added bitterly.

'Is he going to call in the Yard?'

'I don't know what he's going to do', Inspector Playford replied wearily, his tone expressing a whole range of feeling toward his Chief Constable.

'Well, you enjoy your supper and forget about him', said Mrs. Playford, blithely overlooking that it had been she who had introduced the distasteful topic.

A moment later as his first laden forkful of food was half-way to his mouth the telephone rang and news of the fire at Notley's Garage came through.

'I hope you told them you were going to have your supper first', his wife said truculently as he came back into the room from answering it.

'I shall have to go at once', he replied with a sigh. 'Someone's been burnt to death and they suspect foul play.'

'I don't see that a few minutes is going to make any difference and they can't expect you to go on for ever without a proper meal.'

He shrugged his shoulders resignedly.

'No, I'd better go now. Put it on one side for me and I'll have it when I get back.'

'And when will that be? About four o'clock in the morning I suppose', she said in disgust.

'I'll give you a ring within an hour and let you have an idea whether to wait up for me.'

She accompanied him to the front door and gave him an affectionate kiss. Their marriage having been, to their common sorrow, a childless one, she had been pleased to devote all her energies to looking after her husband and, just as important, endeavouring to make him do the same for himself. Her frequent though unavailing efforts to deflect him from the strict path of duty in the interest of his health were a feature of their life which had surprisingly never become diminished.

She gave a final wave as he backed the car out on to the road and drove off.

By the time he reached Notley's Garage, the fire had been extinguished and apart from a uniformed constable standing silently in the shadow of a petrol-pump, everything appeared to be normal. He parked the car by the side door and entered. Inside he found Detective-Sergeant Whiteside, a uniformed sergeant and two more constables. The fire brigade Chief Officer was also there. They were standing together in a group obviously waiting for him.

The floor was awash and the showroom cars had been man-handled to the far end where they stood herded like cattle. But far more sinister than the visual signs of disorder were those that assailed the nose. Through all the reeking fumes inevitably associated with a fire, there came also the unholy smell of burnt human flesh. Playford noticed it as soon as he approached the entrance to Tom Notley's office. Sergeant Whiteside was a pace behind him.

'There he is', he said, waving a loose hand toward the blackened lump that lay in the middle of the floor. 'Bit overcooked for my fancy.'

Inspector Playford was affronted by such a lack of respect for the dead and indicated by his expression that he regarded the remark as being in deplorable taste. It was the same sort of expression he put on when anyone told him a particularly coarse joke and it came as instinctively to his features as the grimace which accompanies a mouthful of persimmon. But Sergeant Whiteside with his bovine mind was incapable of understanding such sensitivity of feeling and never wasted any time in analytical study of his Detective-Inspector's reactions.

Playford stood in the doorway and looked slowly around the small room, keeping his eyes averted from the body on the floor. Then he turned to the fire brigade officer.

'Well?'

'He must have been caught like a rat in a trap, the poor sod. He was locked in and incinerated.'

'Locked in?'

'Look, there's the key in the lock on the outside. That's how we found it.'

'How did the fire start?'

'Having locked him in, someone thoughtfully emptied this four-gallon can of petrol under the door. It was a very simple manoeuvre since, as you can see, the office floor is a step lower than the showroom one.'

Playford looked thoughtful. Then he said:

'But if the petrol was ignited this side of the door, why didn't the flames run back into the can, instead of setting the office alight?'

'I can't tell you that for sure at the moment, but I'm pretty certain that the petrol wasn't ignited in the way you mean. I believe it was set off by the electric fire in the office.'

Playford remembered the small one-bar fire with which Notley warmed his office. It had always looked ancient and dangerous enough without having petrol flowing all about it. As he now peered again, he saw its twisted remains close to the body.

'So that's how it was done,' he said reflectively and then murmured to himself, 'but, God, what a fiendish death.' Aloud he went on, 'And I suppose he never had time to use the telephone?'

'The murderer foresaw that possibility, sir', Sergeant White-side broke in. 'The wire's been cut here.' He indicated the side of the door outside the office where a frayed piece of flex hung loosely.

'Yes, he didn't stand a chance', said the fire brigade officer. 'Though even if he had been able to get through to us, I doubt whether we could have arrived in time to save him.'

'The fire would have caught as quickly as that, would it?' Playford said.

'The office must have been an inferno in no time. Incidentally, I suppose there was the usual amount of combustible junk lying around?'

Playford nodded.

'Yes, the place overflowed with files, trade journals and loose papers generally.'

The fire brigade officer sighed with the resigned air of one whose efforts to prevent untimely cremation were seldom successful. He said:

'One mercy is that these walls prevented it from spreading to the rest of the premises. If that had happened and it had reached the main petrol storage tanks, the whole building would have gone up in flames and we'd have had a major task on our hands.'

'It might have meant more damage but presumably there would have been no greater loss of life', Playford remarked.

'On the contrary, some of our lads might well have lost their lives.'

Inspector Playford accepted the reproach equably and for the next few minutes made as thorough an examination of the scene as he could without disturbing anything. By the time he had finished, an officer had arrived to take photographs. This was Detective-Constable Kane of the Photographic and Finger-print Department of the Wenley Borough Constabulary, who, despite being its one and only member, always thus styled himself.

'When Kane has finished, shall I get the body taken to the mortuary, sir?' asked Sergeant Whiteside.

Playford nodded.

'And then set about discovering his next of kin?' Whiteside continued.

'Whose?'

'Notley's.'

Inspector Playford gazed sadly at his sergeant.

'What proof have we that it's Notley's body?'

'Well of course it must be . . .' Sergeant Whiteside began to expostulate but stopped suddenly in mid-breath and said almost sulkily, 'Well, who else could it be?'

'Prentice', Playford replied quietly and without hesitation.

CHAPTER SEVEN

'LIKE an outing to Wenley?'

The Assistant Commissioner (Crime) of the Metropolitan Police looked across his desk at Detective-Superintendent Simon Manton as he spoke. Manton, who had no idea that the Chief Constable of Wenley had requested Scotland Yard's help nor even that any particular crime had been committed in his area, assumed an expression of mild expectation.

'Not been following the news?' said the A.C.C. with a smile.

'Evidently not sufficiently, sir.'

'A few days ago a man got blown up in a car. That in itself was fairly unusual but what made it even more remarkable was that he had only that morning been released from prison.'

By this time Manton was nodding his head in recollection of the event.

'You read about it?'

'Yes, sir, but without taking in where it had happened.'

'Well, it was at Wenley. Ever been there? It's in the Midlands.'

'Only through it by train a few times, sir.'

'That's enough for most people. It's not a place to spend one's holidays, though I suppose there are worse towns. Anyway I'd like you and Sergeant Talper to go up there and see what you can do to enhance our reputation.' Manton nodded again and the Assistant Commissioner went on. 'Last night they had a mysterious fire in which someone lost his life. The Chief Constable says he was almost certainly murdered and that the case is linked with the exploding car. They don't seem to have got very far in their inquiries and I gather they keep running into dead ends. Hence his request for our assistance. What's further exited them is that they've not so far been able to identify the body of the person killed in the fire.' Manton's expression became one of mock-despondency and the Assistant Commissioner continued, 'It's not quite as bad as it sounds since the only two characters unaccounted for are the owner of the garage where the fire took place and the chap who was blown up in the car. The Chief Constable says it must be one of them and they hope to make a positive identification reasonably soon.'

He paused and picked up a long thin silver paper-knife with the theatrical air of a great conductor and said pleasantly, 'And that's about all I can tell you. I've said you'll be up there this evening.'

Manton looked covertly at the clock on the mantelpiece. It was ten to one and exactly ten minutes later than the A.C.C. was wont to depart to his club for lunch. The A.C.C. now followed his gaze and with a grunt got up from his desk, dropping the paper-knife as if it had suddenly become red hot. Manton turned to go.

'There is just one further thing,' the A.C.C. said and then paused with a pensive frown before continuing, 'you know who the Chief at Wenley is?'

Manton thought for a moment and slowly shook his head.

'It's Ripley. He used to be the Superintendent in charge of — Division. Got appointed Chief Constable about a year ago.'

'Yes, I remember now, sir, but I've never met him.'

'Good chap and very efficient,' the A.C.C. said graciously, 'but I gather he's shaken Wenley up a good deal since he arrived there and I'm not too sure how you'll find him. He didn't sound very pleased at having failed to solve the case with his own resources and it may be that your tact will be subjected to a fair number of strains and stresses.'

'Thanks for the warning, sir.'

The Assistant Commissioner shrugged his shoulders as he took his bowler hat and umbrella from the cupboard in the corner of the room.

'I always think it's a pity when new brooms start sweeping too vigorously too soon', he said philosophically. 'Anyway, keep in touch and let me know if you want anything. In the meantime, good hunting.'

As Manton walked down the corridor in search of Detective-Sergeant Talper to break the news to him of their assignment, he reflected how lucky the C.I.D. was to have an Assistant Commissioner who beneath a pleasant and deceptively easy-going exterior retained an incisive mind with a remarkable power for quick and correct decision. He had the further inestimable attribute of always supporting his subordinates, except in cases of extreme fatuousness.

Five hours later, Manton and Talper were in conference with Detective-Inspector Playford.

From the beginning the two senior officers took a liking to each other. Manton was impressed by the quiet but solid worth of the provincial C.I.D. man and recognized at once that here was an officer who despite a probable lack of imagination and inflexibility of outlook, could be relied upon to do a thorough job of work and not cut any corners. It also soon became apparent to him that Playford was by nature a follower rather than a leader and had no aspirations toward the honour and glory which might follow the successful conclusion of a major criminal investigation. In brief, he lacked ambition. Playford for his part saw in Manton someone whose leadership he was content (even relieved) to accept and in whom he could happily repose full confidence.

Detective-Sergeant Talper sat silently in the background listening as Inspector Playford retailed the chain of strange events which had set Wenley humming with rumour. He and Manton had worked together on a number of cases both in and out of London and so far as he, Talper, was concerned, long might the partnership continue.

'Well, Mr. Manton, that's the story to date', Playford said finally. 'I expect you've got a lot of questions as I'm afraid I've probably not explained everything you want to know.'

'There are a few things', Manton replied agreeably. 'First, tell me some more about this car incident which took Prentice to prison. It was Miss Jason's car?'

Playford nodded.

'Parked outside her office unlocked and with the ignition key in position?' Manton continued.

'That's right.'

'What sort of car was it?'

For a moment Inspector Playford looked nonplussed, then

he furrowed his brow, and after brief hesitation, said, 'A Hillman Minx coupé of pre-war vintage. It was either a 1938 or 39 model.'

'Huh-huh, and why was it left so ready for stealing?'

'Miss Jason never used to lock it or remove the key. There was no question of her leaving it like that for the first time that day.'

'I see', Manton said. 'And on this particular day Master Prentice removed it shortly after five o'clock?'

Again Inspector Playford nodded.

'And not very long afterwards crashed into a lamp-post in this street here?' He indicated a point on the town street plan which lay open on the desk.

'That's right, Mr. Manton. He skidded trying to avoid these Boy Scouts as they came trooping out into the road from their hut which you can also see marked on the plan. That was his first misfortune, though he might still have got away with it if Major Irwin Potts had not happened to have been there and to have recognized him.'

'Yes, fate certainly seems to have been against him that day,' Manton said and went on, 'but what I still don't understand is why he took the car in the first place. What was he going to do with it?'

Inspector Playford shrugged his hefty shoulders. 'We've no idea. He wouldn't tell us and no explanation has ever presented itself. Despite that, I never regarded it as a real case of stealing and it was one of the reasons we were willing to have it dealt with under Section 28 of the Road Traffic Act.' Manton appeared so dismayed by this unhelpfulness that Playford was constrained to add, 'I'm sorry, Mr. Manton', in a tone of genuine apology.

'Do his previous convictions include anything of a similar nature?'

'Car stealing?'

'Yes.'

'No, though there was an occasion when he was working for Notley and took one of his cars. Notley reported it to us as having been stolen and then when he found who'd taken it, he declined to prosecute and became most obstructive.'

'Did Prentice still remain in his employ after that?'

'Oh yes, for several months. It's difficult to know but I rather think that Prentice finally left of his own free will.'

'And for what purpose did he take the car then?'

'It was a case of pure and simple joy-riding. At least that's what Notley said afterwards.'

Manton decided that there was no object in pursuing the topic further at this stage though it might be worth taking up again later. Whether or not it would ever pay a dividend would remain to be seen. It was however already clear from what Playford had told him that the case comprised a mass of complicating undercurrents.

He leant forward resting his forearms on the edge of the desk and said:

'Obviously the first thing we want to know is whose body was found at Notley's Garage. Till it's been identified we can't begin to direct out inquiries. Agreed?'

'Yes, Mr. Manton. I see it this way. If the body turns out to be Notley, we shall then have to intensify our search for Prentice since everything will point to him as the murderer. It must have been something like this. For some reason Notley decided to kill Prentice but his plan misfired and Prentice was only injured. Prentice then realized that his life was in danger – in fact it was I who rubbed this in to him to try and make him talk but without success – and resolved to kill his would-be murderer as an act of self-protection.'

'Or out of revenge.'

'That too. Notley's death would quench a host of motives.'

'But supposing the body turns out to be Prentice?'

'In that event we shall have to look for Notley and the very fact of his disappearance assumes great significance. In fact, if it's Prentice who has been killed, I would say that Notley is more obviously the murderer than if it's the other way round.' He paused a moment to observe Manton's reaction but learnt nothing and continued, 'Furthermore it's not difficult to imagine how it happened. Prentice went to visit Notley and the two men came face to face for the first time since Prentice came out of prison. Prentice threatened Notley. Notley retaliated with force, knocked Prentice out – he's physically by far the tougher of the two – and then set fire to him in his office and disappeared. I'm pretty certain it'll turn out to be something along those lines. What do you think, Mr. Manton?'

'It could be', Manton said cautiously. 'But if so, answer me these questions before we attempt any further reconstructions. If it was Notley who tried to blow up Prentice, why on earth did he use one of his own cars? Surely that was an extremely crude piece of self-incrimination. Then if it is Prentice who has murdered Notley, why did he walk straight into the lion's den by going to see Notley? Particularly as he had every reason for thinking Notley was out to get him. If however it is Notley who has murdered Prentice, why did he also destroy his own property?'

Nobody said anything and Manton went on, 'There are three puzzles for a start. I'm not saying there mayn't be a perfectly simple answer to each. That, I hope, we shall find out in due course.' He noted Inspector Playford's somewhat crestfallen expression and added, 'I entirely agree, Inspector, that in considering the case from the point of view of probabilities and possibilities you have suggested the most likely explanations. I was merely making the point that they're not without their apparent inconsistencies.'

'Human nature', Playford said with the pleased air of a conjurer producing a twin-headed rabbit out of a thimble.

'What about it?' asked Manton in surprise.

'It always accounts for the inconsistencies. So often we try and rationalize an accused's conduct and forget that he's just another human being whose acts are determined by a tangled mass of uncontrolled emotions. The chemistry of the human body is one of life's most complex mysteries', he concluded sententiously.

'There's something in what you say', replied Manton noncommittally. He was intrigued by the Wenley officer's unexpected display of psychological insight and acknowledged the truth of his original premise. The endeavour to rationalize human behaviour was the perennial passion of lawyers, especially prosecuting counsel who were wont to loop the loop in their efforts to provide a reasonable explanation for every fact so that they could present a neatly-packaged case to a Court. He continued, 'Anyway, all this is so much profitless speculation since we've agreed that we can't start any line of inquiry until the body has been identified. Let's get back to something more positive. For instance I'd like to know a bit more about the Notley–Eileen Potts set-up. How far did their association go and to what extent was it known in the town?'

Inspector Playford clasped his hands together slowly and gave the impression of an elder about to preach his monthly sermon on Sodom and Gomorrah. He said:

'It was almost certainly adulterous. Knowing Tom Notley as I do – did – I'm sure he wouldn't have spent so much time on Eileen Potts if she'd declined to lie in his bed. Though he's a ruthless type who is used to beating aside all opposition and getting his own way, on the odd occasion when he has found something too tough for him, he's followed the good old military practice of disengaging with minimum loss and delay.' He paused and added in a tone of disgust. 'But so far as women are concerned, he's always had complete walkovers. I just wouldn't like to begin to estimate the number of girls he's seduced in that flat of his.'

'What type of girls?'

'Anything feminine and preferably fluffy. He wasn't particularly choosey and they almost used to line up outside his door awaiting their turn. All he had to do was admit them one at a time.'

'Sounds fairly unsubtle to me.'

'They weren't interested in subtlety', Playford replied with scorn. 'All they wanted was to wallow in his champagne and giggle at his animal approaches while the gramophone churned out so-called seductive music. As far as I can make out it was always one of those current glamour boys whose nasal noises make apparently sensible girls act like a herd of Gadarene swine.' Manton was about to comment on the inappropriateness of the background music, but Inspector Playford seemed carried away by his role of Savanarola and continued, 'Several times we had to warn him because angry parents were complaining and once we got as far as interviewing a fifteen-year-old girl who'd spent an evening at his flat. But nothing had happened', he added despondently.

'But how did Mrs. Irwin Potts fit into this scarlet picture?' Manton asked quickly, before the denunciation could be continued.

'Ah', Playford said significantly.

'She seems to have been totally different from his usual female company', Manton hurried on, determined to keep the discussion in rein. 'She was married and also a lot older.'

'And what's more there's nothing fluffy about her', added Playford.

'How come then?' Almost before the words had left his mouth, Manton knew the answer he was going to get.

'Human nature again', Playford said in the same satisfied tone as the previous occasion he had trotted it forth as an explanation of the otherwise inexplicable. 'Just one of those things', he murmured.

Manton could have wished that their discussion didn't so often get becalmed in platitudes, but he realized that the provincial C.I.D. man was one of those who had to be left to tell a story in his own way.

'She's a woman in the early thirties; I suppose about thirty-two or thirty-three', Playford began again after a reflective pause. 'She's the tall, willowy sort; wears spectacles and apart from a faintly sick-bed smile never shows any emotion. But' – and here he paused again to ensure his audience's attention for another well-worn adage – 'there was never a truer saying than still waters run deep. How Tom Notley ever came to see anything in her or she to be attracted by him, one will never know. They're the last two people one would have thought of in bed together. She's not his type of woman and he's. . . .' He let the sentence trail away with a shrug.

'As you've said, there's no accounting for human nature', Manton said briskly. 'Every day the most unlikely couple, do the most unlikely things together.' He accepted the Notley–

Potts affair as such and felt no need to philosophise about it.
'How long have the Potts been married?'

'Since just after the war.'

'About ten years then. And how long did this infatuation last?
I said "did" because I gather it's now over.'

'If not over, very much on the wane. No, it *is* over by now',
Playford added immediately. 'At a guess I say it lasted about six
months. Most of last winter and a bit more.'

'Any idea which of them first started to tire of things? Or
was there a break-up by mutual agreement?'

'Far from it. It was common knowledge that it was he who
brought matters to a head, the final bust-up coming about last
Whitsun, so rumour hath it. Though it had lasted much longer
than most of his love affairs, he then completely reverted to type
and took on a cuddly blonde who served at the biscuit counter in
Woolworths.'

'How did Mrs. Potts take it?'

'I doubt whether anyone knows that, but I guess pretty badly.
When her sort falls, they usually fall the whole way and inevitably hurt themselves.'

'And what about her husband? What was his attitude to his
wife's dalliance with Notley?'

Inspector Playford drew in a deep breath and expelled it in
short noisy blasts.

'He's so wrapt up in public life, I'm not sure how much he
notices what goes on in his own home. In addition to being a
J.P. and a borough councillor, he's recently been adopted as
parliamentary candidate for this constituency. He hasn't a
hope of getting in, but it all means endless work.' He made
another breathy sound and continued, 'He must have known
that something was going on, but I suspect he had no idea that it
had reached such serious proportions.'

'From what you say, Mrs. Potts must have been an almost
permanent grass widow. It's often the way marriages start to go
on the rocks.'

'Precisely, Mr. Manton, and as in most of those cases so in
this. I guess that Potts was relieved to have his wife off his hands
for so much of the time and I doubt whether he even bothered to
find out how she was amusing herself or with whom. He just
assumed she was playing prettily in the garden all by herself.
When he finally cottoned on, it was almost too late.'

'Almost?'

'Well, there hasn't been a divorce and they still live under the
same roof.'

'Thanks not to Potts or his wife but to Notley who got fed
up with her.'

'True.'

47

Manton said:

'I'm surprised that in a town of this size with all its gossipy chit-chat, Potts didn't learn quite early on that his wife's relationship with Notley was probably adulterous.'

'Oh, I don't know, Mr. Manton. After all I'm only assuming it was such because of my knowledge of Notley. Gossip never got as open as that. They always behaved themselves perfectly properly in public. It was simply that they used to be seen dining together at various hotels in the neighbourhood with noteworthy frequency. And when I say "dining" I mean it. They always had all the trimmings like cocktails and wines and even liqueurs.' Manton could well imagine that in Wenley such bibulous extravagances would be bound to attract special attention. Playford went on, 'The head waiter at one hotel – a place about seven miles out – told me that they never had the set dinner but used to order stuff like caviare and smoked salmon and special soufflés. Personally you can keep all those fancy things so far as I'm concerned and I don't regard them as proper food for a man; but the point is you don't get them for nothing and you don't eat them on just ordinary occasions – not with all that wine as well.'

It seemed reasonably clear to Manton that Notley and Eileen Potts had misconducted themselves, and that everyone knew this (or could have known if capable of simple arithmetic) except, as usual, the cuckolded husband. He said:

'By the way, how does Potts earn his living?'

'He has a small and not very successful timber business. It's not successful because he never gives it any attention. He has a so-called manager looking after it for him; but he's only a jumped-up labourer and, I suspect, cheats him right and left.'

'What does he use for money then?'

'I suppose he must get something out of the business, but his wife is the one with the money. She was an only child and her father left her a tidy little fortune when he died about eight years ago. It wasn't long after they'd got married. The old boy had been ailing for some while.'

'How much did he leave her?'

'Around eighty thousand pounds; and that after the Chancellor had had his cut. He was a wily old man. Made a packet buying and selling property at the right times.'

'Has Potts got any private means?'

Playford shook his head.

'No. His father owned a small garage business. It was quite a humble affair and he did everything himself. He was a first-class mechanic but had no business sense and he sold it for a pittance when he retired just before the war. He died shortly after.'

'Tell me, what are the respective ages of these three?'

'Potts must be around forty-three or forty-four. His wife's about ten years younger and Notley's somewhere in between the two of them.' He squinted up at the ceiling and concluded, 'Yes, he's just about thirty-eight.'

'One more thing', Manton said, shifting his position in his chair. 'As I understand it when you visited Prentice in hospital the day before yesterday he was so bandaged up as to look like a cocoon. Yet twenty-four hours later he's able to walk out of the place and vanish without trace.'

'I know, I know', Playford said, nodding vigorously. 'But it's not the first time it's happened. I don't mean someone disappear in those circumstances, but I remember there was a fellow involved in a car smash a few months ago and when I went along to see him in hospital, you couldn't see his head for bandage. They must have wound yards of it round him: he looked just like a snowball. Well, two days later I happened to see him in the street and all he then had to show for his accident was a tiny piece of sticking-plaster on his forehead.

'You've got to remember, Mr. Manton, that Prentice didn't have any broken bones or deep wounds and the day he disappeared all he had in the way of dressings was one on his backside. They'd pumped a lot of these new drugs into him and though he can't have been very comfortable, there was nothing to stop him moving. It's true he may have looked as though he'd been engaged in a street brawl, but that's not a too unusual sight in Wenley.'

'Yes, I imagined that was the explanation. One of the features of modern medicine seems to be that people can be almost dead one day and the next be rushing around like a flurry of Foreign Ministers. Nevertheless, as you say, he can't be all that comfortable and it might be worth making a check at local chemists to find out if any of them have sold any of the materials he would require for fresh dressings.' He straightened his back and stretched out his arms. Then, stifling a yawn, he studied the face of his wristwatch for several moments. 'Do you think it's worthwhile phoning the mortuary to find out if they've identified the body yet? I'd like to have that information before we go to bed tonight.'

Dr. Nation did say he'd ring as soon as he could tell us anything and I've got Detective-Sergeant Whiteside down there with him; but I'll certainly give him a call if you like, Mr. Manton.'

'It can't do any harm.'

'Of course we may have to wait till the lab. have had an opportunity of analysing various samples taken from the body.'

'Yes, but the sooner they can give us some idea who it is, the better. Positive proof can follow later.'

Inspector Playford got up and left the room. Manton turned to Detective-Sergeant Talper.

'An interesting set-up, eh, Andy?'

'It is indeed, sir. I must say I'm looking forward to meeting these Potts' and Notley too if he isn't the body in the mortuary.'

'And I'm looking forward to making the acquaintance of Augustus Jason', Manton said, his bright blue eyes fixed on Talper's face. 'He sounds just like a large, cunning spider whose web has endless ramifications. Why did he defend Prentice on a charge of stealing his daughter's car? That's one of the queerest pieces of professional conduct that's ever come to my notice. And why did he try and take out a summons for assault against Notley? Quite extraordinary behaviour by a solicitor in respect of one of his clients. Also why was he (and Potts too) so obviously thrown into confusion when news of Prentice's disappearance from hospital came through?'

Sergeant Talper pondered each question with a deepening frown and Manton continued, 'So far, Andy, Mr. Augustus Jason definitely has my money for being the most interesting character in this story. Watch him carefully and I think you'll find that he will positively radiate leads. Most of them will probably be false, but a few may be genuine.' His eyes glinted with the prospect of battle as he concluded, 'My guess is that he will turn up in this investigation with all the sulphurous frequency of the demon in an old-fashioned pantomime.'

CHAPTER EIGHT

By the time Inspector Playford returned to his office some ten minutes later, Manton and Talper had lapsed into silence. Talper sat at contemplative ease, his mind nowhere in particular, like a chauffeur who has become inured to a lifetime of patient time-killing. Manton on the other hand strolled about the room, peering with half-interest at the framed photographic groups which adorned the walls, while he thought back over their recent discussion.

He had never before seen in one room so many different photographs of police officers desporting themselves in such a variety of ways and he was intrigued by the ease with which he could always pick out Inspector Playford in each group. It didn't matter whether he appeared in football kit (a 1930 group), full uniform for inspection by King George VI (1939 vintage) or black tie and boiled shirt (one of those photographs where a galaxy of heartily beaming faces stare straight into the camera lens); in each, and several others besides, he was completely himself. Indeed he put Manton in mind of a bad character-actor who, despite frantic changes of costume, remains unmistakably and depressingly the same.

As he now returned to the room, both Yard officers looked across at him expectantly. He shook his head.

'No news, I'm afraid, Mr. Manton. I've just been phoning from downstairs. Dr. Nation won't commit himself yet. He's removed the jaws intact and I'll have them sent along first thing in the morning to Notley's dentist to see if he can identify the teeth from dental charts. If they're not Notley's, then presumably they're Prentice's.' He stopped suddenly and after a moment's concentrated frowning went on, 'I'm trying to remember whether Prentice had false teeth, but the more I think about it the more I can persuade myself either way.'

'Why can't the dentist examine the teeth tonight?' asked Manton.

Inspector Playford looked shocked.

'But it's after half past nine', he said. 'His place is all shut up.'

'Can't he be reached at home?'

'You don't know Mr. Golightly. Once he gets home in the evening, he stays there come hell or high water. He recently married his receptionist; darned pretty girl she is too.'

'But, dammit, this is urgent. Twelve hours delay could make all the difference.'

'You phone him yourself if you like, Mr. Manton, but I know the answer you'll get. It'd take more than someone else's murder to budge him.'

Manton tossed his head in exasperation.

'Very well then, if we can't do anything more along that line, we'd better get down to Notley's Garage.'

This time Inspector Playford appeared even more shocked.

'Now?' he asked incredulously.

'Certainly. Why not?' Manton replied with a noticeable edge to his tone.

'I just thought you'd probably prefer to wait till the morning', he said with a faint air of melancholy.

'The morning will bring a fresh batch of problems. Anyway what would your Chief Constable think if, having called in the Yard, the first thing we did on arrival was to go off to an early bed?'

Playford didn't trust himself to make any reply to this, though his expression was more powerful than any words could have been.

Though the garage had been open to normal business that day and, indeed, had enjoyed a fantastically brisk trade in the

51

sale of single gallons of petrol and of such minor necessities as washers and split-pins, Tom Notley's own office had been locked and guarded by a uniformed constable who had kept the endless stream of goopers at a respectable distance.

As Playford led the way through the showroom, the young constable then on duty stepped out of the shadows to meet them.

'Evening, sir. Thought you might be along again', he said tactfully.

'Evening, Pearce', said Playford. 'This is Detective-Superintendent Manton of Scotland Yard and this is Detective-Sergeant Talper, also from there.'

P.C. Pearce saluted Manton who said pleasantly, 'Rather a lonely vigil, eh?'

'Better than what I was on last night, sir. Spent half of that squatting in a blinking hen-house waiting for a thief who never turned up. If he's ever caught, I'd like to wring his neck together with all them cackling birds.'

Manton laughed and said:

'Well, let's have a look at this office.'

The door was unlocked and P.C. Pearce fetched a small mobile searchlight and directed the beam into the room. This succeeded in casting strange illusive shadows which made the scene an even more bizarre one. Twenty-four hours after the event there was also a subtle difference in the combination of smells which accosted the nose. That of burning was slowly being absorbed in the less dramatic but more persistent odour of sodden desolation.

Manton paused on the brink peering in for several moments before carefully stepping down into the office.

'Can you bring that lamp inside?' he said, speaking over his shoulder.

Playford and Talper followed him into the confined space. After gazing intently about him for a while, Manton went on, 'Been through the contents of the safe yet?'

'Not thoroughly', Playford replied. 'I had a quick look at some of the stuff this morning, but I didn't examine anything in detail.'

'Let's have a squint at it now, then.'

Inspector Playford brought from his coat pocket a small key to which an enormous identifying label had been tied and unlocked the safe.

P.C. Pearce stepped forward with a torch and plunging his hand in Manton extracted a large green metal cash-box.

'I haven't opened that yet', Playford said as Manton deposited it on a relatively undamaged corner of Notley's desk.

'Got a key for it?'

Playford again fished in his pocket and this time brought to view a large ring of keys. 'One of these should do the trick', he said.

To be precise, the second one did.

In the top tray was about fifty pounds in cash, but Manton was not concerned with this. Lifting the tray out, he picked up a bundle of letters, loosely tied with a piece of coarse string. There were eight in all, each in the same handwriting and each bearing a Wenley postmark.

Having quickly scrutinized the envelopes, he extracted the letter from the first and unfolded it. As he did so, Playford said:

'That's the Potts's address. These letters must have been written by Eileen Potts.'

The two officers peered over Manton's shoulder as he read it. It was dated early January and turned out to be an ordinary love-letter containing the usual sentiments expressed with an inevitable profusion of high-flown superlatives. Reading it now was rather akin to eating cold rice-pudding and to anyone other than hardened police officers, it would in addition have been embarrassing.

Each of the seven remaining letters proved to be similar in tone and from them it was a simple inference that Tom Notley and Eileen Potts had, as Inspector Playford put it, 'gone the whole hog'.

'It's clear that *he* was also writing *her* letters', Manton said as he folded the last one up and put it back in its envelope.

'Can't understand these love-birds', Sergeant Talper suddenly said. 'It seems they can spend practically every waking (and sleeping) minute in each other's company and still find the need to write these mawkish screeds. Beats me, really it does. It takes me all my time to write one letter a year to my married sister in New Zealand.'

'You're not a romantic, Andy', Manton said. 'You don't know what love can drive you to.'

''Tisn't love, sir. It's just raw passion.'

'Very powerful, too', said Manton dryly. 'However, in addition to leaving us in no doubt about the nature of their association, these letters also tell us something about its course. It's obvious that during the period they cover which is January to the end of March, things were at fever-heat all the time. What I'd like to know is whether she wrote him any letters after he'd started to backslide and, if so, where they are.' He riffled the letters thoughtfully and went on, 'Whitsun. Let's think, it fell about the middle of May this year, didn't it? And it was Whitsun when they're supposed to have had their final bust-up. That means that between the end of March and the middle of May, Notley was fast losing interest. Pity there aren't any letters of that period.'

'I don't suppose she was writing any to him then', Playford said.

'Don't you believe it', Manton replied. 'If she was still trying to hold him I bet she used every means at her disposal, including the written word. Her letters would provide the spearhead or the reinforcement of the pleas she would have been making at their presumably not very joyous meetings.' He turned back to the safe. 'What else have we here?' Thrusting his hand to the back, he drew out a book and held it up to the light. '*Modern Accounting Methods For Business Men And Executives,*' he read out, adding, 'pretty forbidding title.'

'Why keep it in the safe?' Talper said.

'Why keep it at all?' Playford asked.

'Perhaps the contents are more stimulating than the title leads one to suppose.' As he spoke, Manton removed the dust jacket and let out a highly expressive 'Ah.' He held the book out to Playford and Talper with a grin. It had a soft grey cover and looked like an ordinary exercise book. On the outside was a white label which bore the legend SYLVIA SLIPS AGAIN. Beneath this in smaller letters was the further legend, THE TERRIFYINGLY FRANK AND BURNING STORY OF A YOUNG GIRL ALONE IN TANGIER, WRITTEN BY HERSELF.

'Burning story', Playford snorted. 'It's a piece of clotted filth only fit for burning. Most of the copies have been. You can see it's one of those crudely-printed affairs, run-off on a hand-press in some squalid cellar. It also happens to be one of the books we prosecuted Prentice for distributing about a year ago.'

'What happened to him?' Manton asked, obviously interested.

'He was heavily fined.'

'First offence?'

'Yes. We'd long suspected he was the chap who was disseminating such stuff round the town but we never had enough evidence to nail him till this particular occasion.'

'Was he a lone operator?'

'He can't have been. He was just an agent for peddling it, but we were never able to find out where it was printed or who else was in the filthy racket.'

Manton flicked over the preliminary pages of the book. 'No printer's or publisher's imprints anywhere, I see. Simply PRINTED PRIVATELY FOR THE CONNOISSEUR. How did people get hold of his books?'

'By answering discreetly-worded advertisements in the local paper and paying through the nose.'

'I don't imagine that our friend Notley paid for his copy, though. What else is there in this Pandora's Box?'

The next items to be taken from the safe were three more pornographic books whose titles Inspector Playford also recalled as belonging to Prentice's stock. Each bore a false and highly respectable dust jacket. Following these came a bundle of official-looking correspondence held in a large clip. The top letter bore the heading, AUGUSTUS JASON & CO., SOLICITORS. It was quite short and was couched in terms of masterly obscurity. It was obvious that the deal to which it several times alluded was one requiring to be written about with considerable caution.

Playford read the letter slowly and handed it back to Manton.

'Those two have undoubtedly been engaged in a good number of questionable transactions togetber', he said. 'Jason will run all manner of risks for his clients provided they're ready to pay enough and Notley is one of those who believes money will buy him everything.'

'It doesn't seem that he's far wrong', Manton observed as he handed the bundle of correspondence to Sergeant Talper. 'You'd better hang on to these, Andy. We'll go through them later.' He turned back to the safe. 'I think that's the lot. No, wait a moment, what's this?' His hand came out holding a small pocket diary, dated the current year. He flicked over the pages, most of which appeared to be clean and unused. 'Whose writing?' he asked Playford, indicating a scribbled entry for the 24th January.

Playford studied the page after the manner of a woman examining herself in a hand-mirror. Finally he said, 'It's Tom Notley's.'

It was one of those cheap little diaries with which people are apt to be showered at Christmas and which, after a few indecipherable and unnecessary entries, are in mid-February at the latest thankfully cast aside and forgotten. This one seemed to be no exception. The entry to which Manton had drawn attention read *Jason 11 a.m.* and was scrawled diagonally across two dates. Another entry for the following week was *P.£50.* Further on again there was what appeared to be a list of measurements which occupied all the space allotted to the third week in February. The next week had odd notes jotted down at random which for the most part were so abbreviated as to be quite meaningless, except presumably to the initiated. Then for the first time came five consecutive days with an entry for each. Starting with Monday they read, *5.41: 5.38: 5.40: 5.42* and *5.40*, the last being Friday's entry.

'Wonder what they refer to', Manton said. 'They're obviously times; but of what?'

He thumbed on, but they were the last entries until he reached a page at the back headed NOTES. On this there was a rough pencilled sketch of what appeared to be a road junction. It was the shape of a Y lying on its side with the prong pointing to the right. On the top side of the tail of the latter about half-way along from the fork was a pencilled blob and above it a

55

scrawled number which looked like *12* but might have been *15.*
Beneath the sketch were two further numbers, *165* and *70*, one
immediately below the other.

'Two hundred and thirty-five somethings', said Manton.
'Unless of course they're not meant to be added up. Anyway
put the diary in your pocket with those business letters, Andy.
We'll want to examine it again later. You've got the love-
letters too, haven't you?'

Talper nodded.

Having emptied the safe, Manton turned his attention to
the desk, at one side of which stood a twisted metal skeleton
which had once been three tiers of wire trays. Of the papers
which they had held, there were left only a few charred fragments and these crumbled and fluttered deskwards as Manton
touched the structure. Immediately beneath it was a heavy
glass paper-weight about the size of a Bath bun. It was scorched
and cracked but otherwise undamaged. Manton lifted it and
disclosed a piece of pink blotting-paper of the same circum-
ference as the paper-weight. It was singed around the edges
and had obviously been part of a sheet, the rest of which had
been burnt in the fire. On it was printed in elaborate capitals
J.P. 9.45 and beside this was a small neat doodle which appeared
to Manton to be someone lying beneath a car in the occupational
pose of a garage mechanic.

'J.P. for Julian Prentice', he said. The other two officers said
nothing and he took an envelope out of his pocket and deftly
shovelled the piece of blotting-paper into it.

After a further brief study of the office, he looked at his watch
and said, 'It's nearly midnight. I think we might call it a day.'

As they trooped out into the showroom, he turned to Playford and added, 'It would be as well to keep a chap on duty
here for the time being.'

'I'll see to it', Playford replied.

When they reached the hotel where Manton and Talper were
booked to stay Playford got out of the car to see them in. The
air was damp and chilly and the good-nights were brief, but as he
turned to go, Manton said, 'Nine o'clock tomorrow morning
and I shall be hammering on that dentist's door.'

CHAPTER NINE

AT that precise hour the next morning, Manton arrived at
Mr. Golightly's surgery prepared, if necessary, to bulldoze his

56

way into the dentist's presence and to stand commandingly over him until he got the information he wanted.

He had barely, however, lifted his finger from the door-bell when the door opened and there appeared before him a white-coated girl whose welcoming smile, though a trifle mechanical, was a brilliant advertisement for her employer's professional skill.

. As soon as he announced himself, she said, 'Come in, will you? I know Mr. Golightly wants to see you.'

She ushered him into an empty waiting-room and vanished, leaving him to enjoy the overpowering smell of floor polish which pervaded it. A moment later she returned and beckoned him to follow her down the corridor.

At the end lay the surgery and in the middle stood Mr. Golightly himself. He was tall, thin and professorial in appearance with a dedicated look about his eyes which was distinctly unsettling in one of his calling.

Almost before Manton was through the door, he started speaking and his voice sounded as though his mouth was crammed with dry biscuits. After his appearance, this came as no great additional surprise.

'I'm glad you've come early otherwise you would have disrupted my list of appointments,' he said, and then, without a pause, went on, 'There isn't the slightest doubt that the teeth I've been asked to examine are Mr. Thomas Notley's. My examination does not permit of any other conclusion. I haven't the time to go into details now but will do so later if you desire. And now if you will excuse me.' He turned to study the appointment book on his desk and, without looking up, said, 'Send in Miss Docherty, Molly.'

Manton feeling somewhat nonplussed by this turn of events managed to say, 'Yes, I'd like more details later. Perhaps. . . .'

'Yes, very well,' broke in Mr. Golightly without turning round and by now rinsing his hands at the small wash-basin in the corner, 'Then bring along your stenographer at six o'clock. Thank you. Good-bye.'

Molly waited at the door with a patient smile set on her face while Manton still hesitated over his departure. He picked up his hat and then with apparent sudden decision said, 'Forgive me, Mr. Golightly, but there is absolutely no doubt about this?'

'What's that?'

'There's no doubt that the teeth you've examined are Notley's?'

'Yes, yes, I've told you so. I hoped it was only the Wenley police who had to be told everything twice. Now do run along, there's a good fellow.'

Manton sighed imperceptibly and turned toward the door. Molly like an escorting destroyer scuttled ahead of him and had the front door open by the time he arrived there. As he went out, she said with mechanical brightness and a total lack of relevance to his visit, 'Well, that wasn't too bad, was it?' Then adding a brisk 'Good-bye' she closed the door before he had an opportunity of replying.

At least I got what I went for, he reflected as he walked down the street to his waiting car, and now we can start searching in earnest for Master Julian Prentice.

On arrival at police headquarters he was told that the Chief Constable had been asking for him. Since the Chief had been out the previous evening when Manton and Tapler had arrived from London, they had not yet met. Inspector Playford now took him along and made the introductions.

'Come and sit down, Superintendent', the Chief said as soon as they had shaken hands. Turning to Playford he added, 'That's all for the moment, Inspector: I'll let you know if I want you.' As Playford went out and shut the door, the Chief nodded toward it and said, 'A human tortoise.'

This unpromising observation didn't seem to call for any response and Manton had no intention of indicating agreement with it. Happily the Chief Constable quickly went on to inquire about various personalities in the Metropolitan Police, though this was obviously done more as an expected formality than from any genuine desire for news.

'So the body has been identified as Notley's, eh?' he said, bringing the conversation round to business. 'Personally I never for one single moment thought it would be anyone else. I told Playford so several times, but he kept imagining all sorts of unnecessary complications. The truth is, of course, that he funked this inquiry from the outset. That's why I had to call you people in.' He fixed Manton with a coldly official stare and said, 'Well, what's your plan of campaign now?'

'Find Prentice.'

The Chief Constable nodded in vigorous assent and said, 'Yes, we'll get the B.B.C. to put out his description and we'll have his face flashed on all the local cinema screens. Furthermore we'll warn all other police forces to watch out for him – and sea and airports as well.' He paused and added, 'Not that I think you'll find he has gone very far away.'

'You believe he's still in the town?'

'I'm sure of it. He can lie up in Wenley far more safely than anywhere else. Without a doubt someone is hiding him and whoever it is had better watch out or I'll slap in a charge against him too when we find Prentice. And I don't mind who it is', he added aggressively. He pulled a watch out of his waistcoat pocket, studied it with the air of importance of the White Rabbit in *Alice in Wonderland* and stood up. 'I must go now. Got to knock a little sense into the heads of the Watch Committee. I'll see you later in the day.'

A few moments later Manton returned to Inspector Playford's room.

'I've just had a phone call from Major Irwin Potts', Playford said as he entered. 'He wants to see us as soon as possible. Says he's got some important information about the murder.'

'Is he on his way here now?'

'No. He wants us to meet him at his solicitor's office.'

'Oh! So I'm going to have the pleasure of meeting Mr. Augustus Jason as well, am I?' Manton said, rubbing his hands. 'But why does he want this interview to be in the presence of a solicitor? Isn't it a bit unusual in the circumstances?'

'Major Potts is one of those people who fancies himself surrounded by advisers and aides', Playford replied. 'It makes him feel more important.'

It was only a five-minute drive to Jason's office and as they got out of their car, Playford drew Manton's attention to the one behind which they had parked.

'That's Miss Jason's: the same one which Prentice took last March.'

Manton walked over to it and peered in.

'She doesn't seem to have learnt her lesson', he said. 'I see she still leaves the ignition key in.'

'She's an independent young lady', Playford remarked as they started to climb the narrow staircase up to the firm's offices.

Inside the main entrance door was a counter labelled IN-QUIRIES and on the far side of it in front of a small telephone switchboard sat a red-haired girl who doubled the role of telephonist and receptionist. She lifted the headphones from her ears and gave Playford a supercilious stare as he leant across the counter and said jovially, ''Morning, Beryl.'

'Do you wish me to tell Mr. Jason you're here?' she asked in an elegant drawl.

'That's the idea, my girl.'

She turned to the switchboard and deftly contrived to manipulate the necessary plugs and switches without any obvious disruption to her knitting, which consisted of a purple scarf of seemingly unlimited length.

'He'll see you now', she said, flicking out a lead and doing a complicated manoeuvre with the knitting-needles at one and the same time. 'You know his office, don't you? Last on the left.'

Thus dismissed they walked along the dingy corridor with its worn-out linoleum till they reached a door with a frosted-glass panel in the bottom right-hand corner of which there was painted in black letters MR. AUGUSTUS JASON. A murmur of voices came from inside and Playford knocked.

'Come in.'

Manton's first impression of Augustus Jason was of someone thoroughly down at heel. His suit was ill-shapen and the jacket and waistcoat were mottled with a generous selection of animal, vegetable and mineral stains. His grubby soft white collar clearly resented having anything to do with his shirt and was trying to break loose from the front stud. It had already managed to cast off its moorings at the back. His tie, which sagged in a dispirited fashion, received a fine coating of ash as he got up from his chair and noisily blew it off the inch of cigarette which stuck straight out of the centre of his mouth.

Manton could barely conceal his surprise, however, when at length his gaze fell on Jason's footwear, for this was a pair of shoes which were not only beautifully polished but obviously expensively hand-made. They automatically drew attention to an exceptionally neat pair of feet whose contrast with the rest of him Manton found most intriguing. It was very plain that he was as fastidious about his footwear as he was indifferent about the rest of his appearance.

His only greeting to Manton was a curt nod of the head accompanied by an inarticulate throat noise. He made no attempt to shake hands with either of them and Manton wondered idly why he had bothered to stand up at all when they entered his office.

Major Irwin Potts showed very little more enthusiasm, though he did come forward and shake hands. As he did so, Manton watched him covertly and decided that he was a worried man. His forehead was deeply creased and he gave the impression of bracing himself to face an ordeal.

When they were all seated, Potts looked at Jason who was in the process of lighting a fresh cigarette from the one he had just finished and gave him what was obviously his cue to open the proceedings. Jason for his part seemed to be wholly indifferent to his client and when at last he spoke it was in an almost off-hand tone.

'Major Potts has something he wants to tell you about the recent affair at Notley's Garage. He also wishes me to be present.' He looked across at Potts and added, 'You'd better go ahead and I'll stop you if necessary.'

Although Jason's voice was soft and without much inflexion, Manton found its effect mildly mesmeric.

Potts cleared his throat and leaning forward looked at each of the officers in turn as if trying to decide which of them was likely to be the more receptive.

'It was the evening before last – the evening of Notley's murder', he began, fixing his gaze on Manton whose ears immediately pricked at the significant mention of Notley's

name. The point was, of course, whether it was assumption
or something more. The body had been identified only an hour
before and apart from the police and Mr. Golightly, there was
but one person who could know for certain that it was Notley.
That was the murderer. As Potts went on it was apparent that he
was not aware of having said anything significant or of having
dropped a fatal brick. He continued, 'The phone rang and when
I answered it a voice asked if I was Major Irwin Potts. I. . . .'

'Excuse me interrupting,' Manton broke in, 'but did this person
use those precise words?'

Potts flushed and said somewhat huffily, 'As a matter of fact
he didn't. If you really must know, he was a good deal less
polite. He said, "Is that Stan Potts?" '

'Thank you', Manton replied. 'And just before you go on;
I gather this was a male voice?'

'It was.'

'Yes, please go ahead.'

'I asked who it was speaking, but he said names didn't matter.
He said he had been wanting to speak to me for some time
but hadn't been able to as he'd been out of reach of the phone.
He then asked me if I had seen Notley recently. I told him
I wasn't prepared to talk to an anonymous stranger and was
about to ring off when he mentioned something about my wife.'
At this point Potts stopped abruptly and swallowed nervously
before continuing. 'He insinuated that Notley and my wife were
seeing each other and. . . . Well, he made a lot of very unpleasant suggestions about my wife.'

'To save your embarrassment, Major Potts,' Manton broke in
again, 'let me say that I know something about that.'

Potts immediately stiffened and said coldly, 'Indeed? I don't
know what you've been told or who has presumed to tell you – '
he glared across at Playford – 'but perhaps you'd better now hear
the truth.

'This bounder, Notley, did try to start a flirtation with my
wife', he began, looking round aggressively as if expecting to
be immediately contradicted. Nobody spoke and he went on:
'Maybe they did even flirt a bit, though it's all over now and
had been for months. This man on the phone said, however,
that I was a classic cuckold and why didn't I go and see Notley
and ask him if it was true or not. The only thing was, he added,
that there now wasn't any time left, which was a pity because
it would have been an interesting meeting.' Potts paused again
and dabbed at his forehead with a folded handkerchief. 'You
can imagine how I was feeling and I simply rang off. A few
minutes later the phone started ringing again and I was so certain
that it must be the same man that I didn't answer it. I just
let it go on until he obviously got tired of receiving no reply

and gave up trying. It seemed at the time, however, as though it would never stop ringing and it was a horrible sensation standing there and knowing this person was doing all he could to get through to me again. It made the silence which followed seem terribly eerie.'

Potts sat back in his chair and eyed in turn the other three occupants of the room. Augustus Jason appeared to be lost amongst his own thoughts behind a veil of cigarette smoke and Playford looked at Manton with an exrpession which clearly said, it's all yours.

Manton thoughtfully wrinkled his nose before speaking.

'What time did you receive this telephone call?' he asked.

'It must have been very shortly after half past nine. I know I switched on the radio to listen to a symphony concert which began at nine-thirty and I had barely heard the opening bars when the wretched set went dead. It was something loose in one of the valve connections and I had just got it going again when the phone rang. It couldn't have been more than three or four minutes later.'

'So it must have been between say nine-thirty-two and nine-thirty-six or seven.'

'Yes, I suppose so', Potts agreed.

'And what was the length of time between your cutting him off and the phone starting to ring again?'

'Not more than a minute or so. Not much longer than it takes someone to dial a number.'

'Have you any idea from where this person was speaking?'

'It was from a public call-box; I could tell that. I heard him press button "A" when I answered. You know the way you can hear the coins drop?'

'Who else was in the house at the time?'

'No one. My wife was out at a meeting and I was alone.'

As he asked his questions and listened to the answers,Manton wore an expression of judicial impartiality which gave no indication of his thoughts.

'Did you recognize the voice at all?'

'No, and I don't think it was disguised. It was fairly ordinary, though it had a nasty insinuating undertone.'

'Any voice can be made to sound that way', Manton observed. Potts said nothing and there followed a further silence which ended by Manton saying, 'And you connect this with the murder at Notley's Garage?'

'It's not my business to connect it with anything', Potts said crisply. 'In view of its possible significance, however, I considered it my duty as a citizen to inform the police of it.

'Now I've done that and if you have no further questions to ask me, I'll be on my way as I've got an important meeting to attend.' He turned toward his solicitor who had sat silent and almost motionless throughout his interview and said in a self-important tone, 'Well, thank you, Jason, for making yourself and your office available.'

'Don't mention it,' Jason replied and with a chuckle added, 'it'll all go down on your bill.'

Potts ignored this somewhat dubious pleasantry and nodding his farewells all round made for the door.

Manton and Playford prepared to follow suit under Jason's watchful gaze. As they were about to depart, he suddenly said, 'It's a long time since we were honoured by having Scotland Yard nosing around our dunghill, isn't it, Herbert?'

'Not since the murder of that prostitute in your road', Playford replied agreeably.

'That's true; even though you do make it sound as if I committed it. I think you should explain to the superintendent that someone was duly convicted and hanged.'

'One of your clients.'

'There you go again, Herbert', Jason said in mock despair. Turning to Manton he went on, 'To hear the Wenley police talk you wouldn't think that anyone other than my clients ever committed any crimes in this town.'

'Well, what's the betting this time?' Playford asked in an unfriendly tone. 'First one of your clients gets blown up in a car, then he vanishes in mysterious circumstances and meanwhile another gets burnt to death in his garage.'

'I soon shan't have any clients left to commit crimes for you, shall I? In any event one of the persons you mention was not a client at the time of his demise.'

'You mean Notley?' Manton broke in.

'I do. He was an ex-client. We had, as Herbert has doubtless told you, severed our professional connection on the day of his death.'

'I note,' said Manton, 'that both you and Major Potts assume that it was Notley who was murdered. There's never been anything official to that effect, you know.'

'Well, wasn't it? It seems obvious that it must be.'

'As a matter of fact it was, but. . . .'

'But we shouldn't make these daring assumptions in case we arouse police suspicions, eh?' Jason interrupted in a heavily sarcastic tone.

'I never said that', Manton retorted quickly.

'All you policemen are the same. It doesn't matter whether you're slick boys from the Yard or local sons like Herbert here.'

Manton decided to put on his blandest smile. He knew Jason was trying to needle him and he was determined not to allow him any success.

'Since you mention Notley, perhaps you'd tell us what brought about his transfer to your ex-list.'

'Listen to him, Herbert. Treats me like an innocent who doesn't know anything about the twisting ways of policemen. "Perhaps you'd tell us", he says sweetly.' Removing a fractional end of cigarette from between his lips and speaking in a quite different tone he went on, 'Well, as a matter of fact I will tell you. We had a row about my daughter. I told him to lay off her or take his business elsewhere. He poked me one in the eye and said he would. He said a good many other things beside, but they're neither here nor there.'

'They might be.'

'Whether they are or not, I'm not telling you', Jason replied curtly.

'What did he come and see you about that morning?' Manton asked.

Jason turned to Playford.

'Never let it be said again, Herbert, that Augustus Jason doesn't co-operate with the police.'

'Oh, you've always been most co-operative when it suited you', Playford replied sweetly.

'Ungrateful flatfoot', Jason murmured and went on. 'He came to see me because he didn't like the nasty suspicions he felt you had formed about him. He was worried lest you should suddenly pounce on him for the attempted murder of Prentice, though he thought he could prove his innocence.' He looked mockingly at Manton and continued, 'Don't get excited, Superintendent, because we never got as far as discussing that. I refused to accept his instructions unless, as I've said, he promised to cease pestering my daughter and that precipitated our row.'

'Did he voice any suspicions?'

'He pretended that he had a very good idea who the person was who had tried to kill Prentice.'

'But no name was mentioned?'

'No, Superintendent, no name was mentioned at all', Jason said in a lightly jeering tone.

'Well, thank you for all your help, Mr. Jason. I don't doubt we'll want to see you again sometime.'

The solicitor threw up his hands in simulated horror.

'I'll lose all my clients if ever they hear I've been thanked by the police for helping them', he said. 'It'll be like the kiss of death on my practice.'

'There's one question I'd like to ask you before we go', Playford said and his tone warned Manton of trouble ahead. 'What news of your precious client, Prentice?'

'News? News?' Jason repeated softly and then said, 'I think I ought to have more notice of that question.'

'Either you've heard from him or you haven't. It's as simple as that.'

'Come now, Herbert, you know I'm not going to discuss my client's affairs with inquisitive policemen.'

'It's different when the client is wanted for murder.'

Jason's face became expressionless and there was an uneasy silence till Manton said, 'What Inspector Playford's saying is that we want to find Prentice since we think he can assist us in our inquiries.'

'Which is exactly the same thing, except that he put it more bluntly and in considerably fewer words.'

It was now clear to Manton that nothing would be gained by protracting the visit and he turned toward the door. Playford gave Jason a final glare and followed him out of the room.

Though Manton decided to make no reference to the local inspector's ill-timed intervention, he fervently hoped that he would in future show more finesse. In any event Jason was the last person upon whom to use such methods.

Half-way down the corridor, Playford, who was a pace or two behind him, stopped and put his ear to the door they were then passing and from the other side of which came the murmur of voices. He listened unashamedly with an intent expression while Manton's embarrassment grew with every moment as he waited for Jason to pop out of his room and catch them.

When Playford finally tore himself away from his listening-post, his expression was suggestive of the cat that has swallowed the canary. He said nothing, however, till they were down the stairs and out on the pavement again.

'Never know what you won't pick up in that sink', he said cheerfully, his recent clash with Augustus Jason apparently forgotten in the excitement of what he'd heard through the key-hole.

'What did you?' Manton asked, trying not to sound over-interested.

'Claudia Jason's was one of the voices – it was her office anyway. The other was a man's and his name sounded like Dominic. Is there such a name?' Manton nodded and Playford continued, 'They both sounded a bit agitated and she suddenly said, "Whatever happens, Dominic, the police must never get to know".'

'She might not have been referring to anything connected with this case', Manton remarked.

Playford shot him a quick look of surprise and said tersely: 'But I'll bet you anything she was.'

CHAPTER TEN

'WHERE now?' Playford asked as they got back into the car.

'First to headquarters for a quick word with Talper and then to Mrs. Potts. Think we shall find her in?'

'We could phone and find out – but I suppose you'd sooner arrive unannounced?'

Manton nodded.

'Yes, it's usually more profitable.'

They found Sergeant Talper about to go out and Manton gave him some hurried instructions. As they afterwards drove off again, Manton referred to their recent interview with Jason.

'He seems to be very much the heavy father where his daughter is concerned. It contrasts oddly with the rest of his outlook on life.'

'He's absolutely devoted to her', Playford agreed. 'His wife died when Claudia was born and he's been both mother *and* father to her – and woe betide anyone who does her any harm.'

'How does she feel about being the subject of such a proprietary interest?'

'I think it irks her. She's a very determined young lady with more than average self-assurance and I gather she has several times made it plain that she intends to lead her life without parental interference. Mind you, I'm sure she's fond of the old man despite finding him pretty tiresome over some things.'

'Do they live together?'

'Yes, in a great Victorian barrack of a house in Wybrow Park: that's on the southern outskirts of the town. It was a very fashionable part just after the first war, but now it has a rather seedy and dilapidated air about it. Nobody has the money to run houses that size these days: or rather the ones that have have built themselves nice modern homes further out.'

'But Jason must have made a good pile of money.'

'He has, but he doesn't spend it on his house. He and Claudia are looked after by an aged crone who used to be Mrs. Jason's nurse, so heaven knows how old she must be now. She's been with the family over fifty years and, come to think of it, the gloomy old house is rather an appropriate setting for her. She's a bit like something out of one of those X films.'

Manton was pondering this when the brakes were viciously applied and he was shot violently forward. Since Inspector Playford's driving had hitherto been of the steady order of a

66

maiden aunt's, he was momentarily annoyed by the unexpectedness of the shock.

'Sorry, Mr. Manton, but this is where Prentice had the accident in Claudia Jason's car. There's the Scout hut', he added, gesturing toward a prefabricated Gothic-style building which stood in a rough field.

Manton refrained from the comment that sprang to his lips when he saw that Playford was blissfully unaware of any irony in the situation.

'Is this the road in which Potts lives?' he asked, swallowing.

'Yes. Their house is on the right about a hundred and fifty yards past that turning.'

A few moments later Playford drew across the road and halted outside a neat modern detached house which was carefully different in style from its neighbours, though it required no expert to spot that all had been built at the same time and by the same builder. On a brick pillar which supported a wrought-iron gate of fussy design was a chaste wooden plaque bearing the name of the house which was BELLAGIO.

'I believe it's a place in Italy or one of those countries', Playford said in a helpful tone, as Manton read it aloud. He went on, 'All the houses in this road have snobby unpronounceable names and their owners were livid when the postal authorities insisted on giving them numbers.'

Shifting his gaze down, Manton now saw beneath the name-plaque a small '12', very much in the position of an unwanted poor relation.

The two men got out of the car and walked up the orange-yellow sandy drive to the front door.

'Someone does a lot of work in this garden', Manton said, observing the neat grass verges, the trim appearance of the flower-beds and the freshly-raked drive itself.

'They have a man four times a week', Playford replied; so promptly that it struck Manton there was apparently very little in Wenley daily life that he didn't know about. An encyclopaedic local knowledge was of course the forte of many police officers and often their greatest asset when it came to investigating crimes.

Playford jabbed a stubby finger at the door-bell and immediately there was one of those synthetic but not unmelodious chimes within. Eileen Potts herself opened the door. Manton thought he detected fleeting alarm in her expression as she recognized Playford but she immediately regained her composure and asked them in.

'I'm sure you'd like some coffee', she said when they were in the drawing-room. 'It won't take me a minute.' She disappeared out of the room without waiting for any answer.

She returned a few minutes later bearing a tray and it was noticeable that she had also taken the opportunity of renovating her appearance. Her hair was tidier and her lips newly reddened.

No one spoke until she had poured out and handed round the cups. Playford immediately made himself at home by sitting down and blowing vigorously on his.

'What is it you want to see me about?' she asked quietly when they were all seated, her eyes darting warily behind her blue-rimmed spectacles.

'I take it you know of Mr. Notley's death, madam?' Manton said.

She shuddered.

'Yes. I've read about it in the local paper.'

'You will appreciate that in an investigation such as the one we're now engaged upon, the police have to dig deep to make certain they obtain every relevant detail.'

'I suppose so', she replied, nervously twisting her wedding-ring around.

'Then you won't be either surprised or I hope distressed by the questions I want to put to you', he said. Watching her carefully, he went on, 'What was your relationship with Mr. Notley at the time of his death?'

For a time the silence was broken only by the gentle sound of coffee being stirred while Eileen Potts gazed abstractedly into her cup.

When she looked up, her expression matched the fierce resentment of her tone as she spoke.

'What's the good of such questions? He's dead now, so why erect him a memorial of mean gossip? And why should I have to endure further torture? Don't you think I've had enough?' She stopped as suddenly as she had begun and, hanging her head, noisily blew her nose in an attempt to stifle her emotions. She lifted her spectacles and dabbed at her eyes with the small twisted handkerchief which had borne the brunt of her feelings. 'All right', she said. 'I know I shan't help myself by banging my head against a wall; I'll try and answer your questions.'

Manton said nothing, but maintained an air of limitless patience. Eileen continued:

'It's true that Tom and I had seen much less of each other during the past few months. We agreed to do that out of fairness to my husband.'

'Out of fairness to your husband?' Manton echoed incredulously.

'Yes. You see he didn't know how Tom and I felt about each other until I told him. I asked him for a divorce and it came as an awful shock to him. He was terribly hurt and refused to consider it. He was absolutely adamant and insisted that I didn't see Tom any more.' She paused and for the first time since she'd started speaking looked across at Manton. Her eyes, despite the nearness of tears, were undisguisedly hostile. She went on, 'When two people loved each other as Tom and I did, you can't just part by slamming a door. You do it gradually like a drug addict whose cure involves decreasing doses – not a complete and sudden privation. So Tom and I saw less and less of each other while the pain wore slowly off.' She fluttered a hand vaguely and added, 'I wonder whether you can possibly understand.'

'I think I can', Manton said, marvelling that anyone could expect him to believe such a piece of pretentious piffle. 'You're being most frank and helpful but you didn't quite answer my question.'

'I last saw him over a month ago. That answers it, doesn't it?'

'Did your husband approve of your continuing to see him?'

'He had to,' she said tartly, and then quickly retrieved herself by adding, 'I mean, that was the arrangement and my husband agreed to it.'

'It has been suggested to me, madam, that you and Mr. Notley had a row last Whitsun which marked the end of your association.'

Eileen Potts laughed nervously.

'Of course if you want to believe every bit of third-hand gossip about us, you'll probably be arresting me any minute for his murder. After all, I've no doubt that my friends are bursting to reassure each other how I did it from the madly-jealous-rejected-mistress motive.' She picked up her coffee-cup, drained the now cold contents and continued, 'Naturally Tom and I had occasional rows but no more than lovers usually have. I can promise you that ours was not an enviable situation. A so-called lovers' idyll doesn't exist outside a vacuum, in case you didn't know that.'

Manton maintained a Chinese impassivity but switching the subject abruptly, said:

'Where were you the evening before last?'

'The evening Tom was killed?' she asked suspiciously, but Manton just stared at her and she went on, 'I was at a meeting of the Recorded Music Society at the Saint Cecilia Rooms.'

'What time did it finish?'

'I don't know. I left before the end. I found the room awfully hot and they played some modern French music which I didn't much care for.'

'Didn't you know in advance what the programme was going to be?'

She looked at him sharply.

'Yes, but not that I was going to dislike it.'

'About what time did you leave?'

'I've no idea. I had a bit of a headache, so walked home to get some air. I arrived back a little before half past ten.'

'And your husband was here then?'

'Yes, he was working in his study.'

'Did you come home direct?'

'Yes, definitely', she replied quickly, but it didn't require a detective to tell that she was lying.

'What did you think of her?' Playford asked when they were driving back to headquarters. 'She doesn't give one the impression of being a passionate woman, does she? Though I know you can't always go by looks.'

'I should imagine,' Manton said thoughtfully, 'that she's a mass of inhibitions beneath that normally placid exterior.' He yawned and added, 'She's not a very accomplished actress either. I wonder why she lied about coming straight home from her meeting. We shall have to check and counter-check times there. Incidentally I've sent Talper along to the telephone exchange to see if he can find any corroboration of Potts's story of the telephone call he received.'

'But Wenley's on automatic.'

'I know. We probably shan't get anywhere but we're bound to follow it up.'

'I've known Eileen Potts for a good many years but I've never seen her so obviously on edge as she was to-day. She's undoubtedly worried about something.'

'Yes, it was interesting', Manton said in a tone of pensive satisfaction. He seemed, however, to be in no mood for further eludication.

Headquarters appeared on their arrival to be deserted; the reason being that it was eleven o'clock and those not out on duty had migrated to the canteen for revitalizing cups of strong tea or mysterious grey coffee.

As the two officers passed the inquiries counter, a young police cadet spoke to Playford.

'There's someone waiting to see you in your office, sir.'

'Who?'

'He wouldn't give his name, sir, but he said you'd be expecting him.'

'He shouldn't have been left alone in my office', Playford said sternly. 'Why didn't you keep him down here?'

The cadet's cheeks flamed with colour.

'I'm terribly sorry, sir, but I thought . . . well, I mean, he more or less said he was a friend of yours and . . . well, sir, he knew which your office was', he stammered unhappily.

Playford turned away and started up the stairs which led to the
C.I.D. offices. He said:

'A decent lad, but he'll never make a policeman. Far too
trusting. He'd be as likely as not to leave the town's biggest
rogue alone in the Chief's room – and then take him a cup of
tea and some magazines to look at.'

He reached the door of his office and flung it open. Suddenly he froze in his tracks, his jaw sagging and his eyes popping
from his head. In a moment of alarm Manton thought he had had
a seizure and instinctively moved forward to catch him before he
pitched to the floor. Then:

'Ah, good morning, Inspector, so you're back at last', said
a suave voice from inside the room.

Sitting at ease in the only decent chair and making no effort
to get up was Julian Prentice.

For several seconds the tableau was maintained: Inspector
Playford staring speechless at his visitor who returned him an
amused and faintly insolent smile. Manton, who found his
entry into the room blocked, squeezed past to go and hang up
his hat and coat. When he turned round, he found Prentice
watching him with mocking eyes. He was about to speak when
Playford recovered his voice.

'What the blazes . . .' he began, when Prentice held up a
deprecating hand.

'Really, Inspector, this is no way to welcome someone you've
been all impatience to see. Now just sit down and relax and think
of all those questions you're bursting to ask.' He looked toward
Manton and smiled conspiratorially. 'You must be the superintendent who has come all the way from Scotland Yard to help
our inspector friend. I think I did read your name in the newspaper but I'm afraid I can't remember it and it doesn't seem as
though we're going to be introduced.'

His tone was designedly offensive and Manton itched to clip
him crisply across the head. This, however, being out of the
question, he said to Playford:

'Let's get down to business. Would you close the door?'

Slowly the inspector came to life. He did as he was bidden
and then sat down beside Manton who had already seated
himself behind the desk. Prentice watched these preliminaries
with the same air of amused insolence and it was abundantly
clear that he was enormously pleased with himself about something. Apart from his appearance, his very visit presupposed
this and it was Manton's guess that the reason for it would soon
emerge.

'What's brought you here?' he said.

71

'Now don't tell me that you, too, are not pleased to see me', Prentice replied in a tone of simulated injured innocence.

'Stop being funny and answer my question.'

Prentice shook his head sadly.

'Oh, you policemen, with your interminable questions', he murmured. 'I have a theory, you know, that in the next life you'll all be put together in a sort of celestial cattle-pen and left to ask each other dreary questions till your harps warp. However, maybe you're not interested in my theories. You want to know why I've come here. The answer is very simple: when last I saw the inspector I told him I'd pay him a visit when I thought I could help him.'

'And in what way do you think you can help?'

'Really, Superintendent, what an extraordinary thing to say. Do you or do you not want to question me; because if not I won't waste any more of my time here?' He made as if to get up but Manton ignored both question and gesture and said:

'Where have you been since you walked out of hospital?'

'Ah, I thought you'd want to know that.' He smiled blandly and went on, 'I've been staying with friends.'

'Who and where?'

'Now surely you wouldn't want me to involve them in this. That would hardly be fair to them, would it?'

'You realize the consequences of refusing to disclose where you've been?'

'I take it you refer to the time-honoured police custom of automatically inferring what's least favourable to anyone? Yes, I realize that – for that matter, who should, better than I?'

'Why did you walk out of hospital without a word to anyone?'

'I found it much too much like the place I'd just come from and once I felt fit enough, I decided to buzz. The inspector will tell you that I've never been one for making a nuisance of myself and so I slipped out without any fuss. Incidentally it was the inspector who was partly responsible – I can see from his look that he has a guilty conscience about it.' Indeed Playford was managing to look a trifle embarrassed at this reminder of his blunt effort to frighten Prentice into talking when he'd visited him in hospital on the day of his admission.

'Did you believe it was Notley who had fixed the car?'

'He was certainly on my short list of suspects.'

'And did you leave hospital because you feared he might make another and more successful attempt at killing you?'

'That was certainly an influencing factor, as I've already told you.'

'What were the other factors?'

'I've told you that too. I just didn't like the atmosphere there.'

'Have you been hiding in the same place all the time?'

'Hiding? I haven't been hiding anywhere. I've been convalescing.'

'At the home of these friends?'

'That's right.'

'Didn't you require any medical attention?'

'Only a little – a little first aid, shall we say.'

'And who provided that?'

'My friends.'

'And what's your condition now?'

Prentice sniggered.

'One of pulverization from so many subtle questions', he said.

'Don't be flippant.'

'No, of course, I mustn't. I'm sorry; I forgot that it's an unforgivable sin when being third-degreed by the police. There are so many things one has to try and remember, you really ought to issue a small handbook entitled, *Correct Conduct For Suspects*. It could comprise a very long list of "don'ts" and just a few "do's" such as: "Do call every policeman, *Sir*", "Do stand up when a policeman enters the room", and "Do make a full confession of your guilt whether you've done it or not".' He stopped and grinned at the two officers. He had a small pursed mouth but when he smiled it opened like a fully-stretched elastic band to reveal a fine range of uneven teeth of varying dirty shades. His appearance was furthermore not improved by his obvious need of a shave and Manton reflected how a stubbly face managed to impart an air of seediness far removed from the manly luxuriance of a full-grown beard.

Easing himself forward in the chair, Prentice put his hands on the arms and heaved himself to his feet. As he stood up, he brushed a powdering of dandruff off his shoulders and a lank strand of hair from his forehead. Then he walked a few paces across the room, about-turned and went back to the chair.

'Does that little demonstration answer your question about my health?' he asked. 'Apart from being sore around the thighs and getting stiff when I've been sitting down, I've made a complete recovery.'

'You're certainly in very different condition from when I say you in hospital', Playford said without any pleasure.

'There's no need to sound so disgruntled about it. Oh, but I seem to remember your expressing regret that I wasn't killed. Still feel the same way?'

Manton had no wish for the interview to be turned into a battle of retaliatory taunts and said quickly:

'Why did you take Miss Jason's car?'

Prentice's expression immediately changed and he looked up sharply.

'This is a very sudden switch', he said in an attempt to gain time.

'Don't stall, Prentice', Manton said sharply. 'We know it wasn't a case of simple joy-riding and we don't believe you intended to steal the car for good, so why *did* you take it?'

'Because I was asked to.'

'By whom?'

'No comment.'

'Asked to take that particular car?'

'Yes.'

'Why?'

'Because it was more takeable than others.'

'And what were you going to do with it if you hadn't had an accident?'

'No comment once more. I know you. . . . No, I've already said enough – maybe too much; but after all I have come here to help you.'

'A fat lot of help . . .' Playford started to expostulate when Manton quickly forestalled him.

'What do you know?' he prompted.

'I know you're often a bunch of bastards.'

'Were you going to hand it over to someone else for them to do something with it?' Manton asked, an idea slowly forming in his head.

'Never mind what I was going to do with it. Just accept that I removed it for reasons other than personal acquisitiveness. Believe me if I ever go in for car-stealing, they won't be ancient rattle-boxes like Claudia Jason's. It'll be "Watch out, Lady Docker".'

'Do you always do everything you're asked to – I mean like taking someone's car without their permission?'

'If it's made worth my while.'

'Ah! so you were paid for the job', Manton said, an early suspicion confirmed.

'Certainly I was.'

Playford rumbled angrily. Prentice looked his way and said:

'It's no good working yourself up into a state of righteous indignation, Inspector. You know as well as I do that the car episode is finished. I've done time for it and there's a cosy legal doctrine called *autrefois convict* which, as you know, means in plain language you can't bloody well be done twice for the same job.'

'No, but if we ever get at the truth, Prentice, I'll bet an honest penny we'll have evidence to charge you with some further offence', Playford said vehemently.

'If.' Prentice blew the small sibilant word back into Playford's face and laughed.

Manton realized that his next question was unlikely to receive an answer but nevertheless decided to ask it for the record.

A refusal to answer any question always preluded someone as slippery as Prentice subsequently proclaiming that he was never asked it.

'Who paid you to take it?'

'Try another line, Superintendent, you've exhausted this one.'

'Do you agree that you had a motive for murdering Notley?'

Prentice's enjoyment of the situation seemed to increase.

'Only one?' he asked.

Manton nodded.

'Yes,' he said, 'self-preservation. You killed him to prevent his killing you.'

'But how can you be sure I didn't do it out of black revenge?' Prentice asked, highly amused.

'Because you haven't the necessary guts', Manton replied equably. 'Your sort is only driven to murder out of fear for your own skins.'

Twin spots of colour appeared on Prentice's pallid cheeks and his eyes took on a mean and angry look. He started to rise from his chair, but Manton said curtly:

'Sit down. I haven't finished yet.'

'You've no right to keep me here.'

'Quite correct, but don't forget you came of your own free will in order to help us poor blundering boobs – and there's still a lot more help I want from you.'

Prentice sank sulkily back into his chair again, his mood now very different from what it had been a few minutes before. He glowered at Manton who went on:

'We know this car was waiting for you outside the prison on the day of your release and that you were expecting it. Who got in touch with you about it?'

'I had a note a few days before I came out', Prentice replied sullenly.

'Who from? Notley?'

'It might have been.'

'Surely you know his writing; you worked for him for some time?'

'It was a typed note.'

'What about the signature?'

'Also typed.'

'But it was Notley's name?'

'Just T.N.'

'Have you still got the note?'

''Course I haven't.'

'Why not?'

He stared at Manton as though he were half-witted before replying.

'Because, Mr. Superintendent, one doesn't keep certain letters in prison.'

'Did it come by ordinary post?'

'Are you joking? Of course it didn't.'

'Smuggled in, you mean?'

'*You* said it.'

'I see', Manton murmured to himself, then he went on. 'What exactly did the note say?'

'Look, for Pete's sake', Prentice cried out testily. 'How much more of this? Which? Why? What? Who? You're making my ruddy head swim with all your lousy questions.'

'Come on, don't put on an act', Playford said sardonically. 'Just answer the question. What was in this note?'

Prentice looked at him malevolently and Manton couldn't help reflecting how the two of them seemed to act as catalysts on each other.

'It was a very short note', Prentice muttered surlily. 'It just said to expect a car when I got out.'

'And it gave you particulars? Where it would be parked, etc?'

'Yes.'

'Any instruction about where to go, or how and when you were to return it?'

'It said I should come and see him as soon as possible.'

'At his garage?'

'It didn't say where.'

'No, I can imagine it was fairly craftily worded, but that's what you understood?'

'That is what I understood', Prentice sneered.

Whether or not Notley was the originator of the note, Manton was not surprised that it contained the minimum data whereby its author might be traced. In any event he would have known that Prentice would destroy it after reading. And if by any chance it had fallen into wrong hands, little harm would have been done. For example, supposing the police had ever got to tackling Notley about it, he would have lost no time in pointing out that someone had obviously tried to incriminate him by typing his initials on it. All this passed swiftly through Manton's mind before he asked his next question.

'Did you get in touch with Notley after you came out of prison?'

'Yes', Prentice said slowly after a thoughtful pause.

'How and when?'

'I spoke to him on the telephone the day before yesterday.'

'You never saw him?'

'No.' There was now a touch of defiance in his tone.

'Were you planning to see him?'

The question was asked in a casual voice, but it made Prentice look at Manton suspiciously before replying.

'I should probably have seen him if he hadn't got killed.'

'Did you have any fixed appointment to visit him?'

Again Manton found himself the subject of a long searching stare before Prentice answered. The stage had now been reached where he clearly wished to ascertain the extent of Manton's knowledge before committing himself. Though no poker-player, Manton had been a detective for long enough to be able to conceal his hand from unwanted eyes and he had no intention of satisfying Prentice's curiosity in this instance.

'No', Prentice said with sudden decision.

'Quite sure about that?' Manton asked agreeably.

Prentice took a deep breath.

'Quite', he said.

'Notley was killed shortly after nine-thirty the evening before last. Would you care to say where you were then? You don't have to answer if you don't want to.'

A slow artful smile spread across Prentice's face.

'But certainly I'll answer', he said, all his confidence apparently restored. 'Between nine and ten that evening I was with someone all the time.'

So that's why you're so pleased with yourself, Manton thought. Aloud he said:

'Where?'

'At his home.'

'Doing what?'

'Discussing a business matter.'

'And he, of course, will corroborate this?'

'Ring him up if you don't believe me.'

'Who?' Manton asked formally, though he guessed the answer before it was given. This, he now realized, was the moment Prentice had been waiting for with ill-concealed patience. When Prentice spoke, his voice embodied a lifetime's contempt for the law and its officers.

'Augustus Jason,' he said in jeering triumph.

CHAPTER ELEVEN

PRENTICE hummed cheerfully but tunelessly as he climbed the stairs to Jason's office. He nodded at Beryl, whose knitting more than ever resembled a giant strip of purple ecto plasm and started to walk down the corridor.

'Here', she called out after him. 'You can't go barging in like that.'

He stepped back a pace and winked at her round the corner of the wall.

'He'll want to see me', he said airily.

'Maybe he will, but just wait till I find out.' Her hand shot out with the deftness of an ant-eater's tongue and after a moment she said, 'Mr. Prentice is here. Will you see him, Mr. Jason?'

An inarticulate monosyllabic sound came down the line and she turned back to Prentice.

'Yes, you can go along now', she said in the reproving tone of a schoolteacher releasing a small pupil from detention.

Prentice thought of replying but instead just winked at her again. It was a peculiarly suggestive wink which he guessed would annoy her more than any words. As she turned away in disdain, he cast her a final lecherous look and padded off down the corridor.

As he was passing Claudia's office, the door opened and she appeared. She was reading a document and didn't at first notice him.

'Oh, it's you', she said with a start as she almost bumped into him and immediately began to beat a retreat.

'How's the boy-friend?' Prentice asked with a grin.

'I don't know what you mean', she replied loftily and began to shut the door.

'That young chap you've been seeing recently – Dominic something or other. Looks quite a decent fellow: better than your late elderly beau, eh?' He cocked his head on one side. 'Late? That's rather apt, isn't it?' he sniggered, quite undismayed by her icy reception of his remarks. 'Good riddance all round there, I'd say, wouldn't you?' But by this time he found himself standing alone in the corridor facing a firmly-shut door and with a shrug of his shoulders, he moved along to Jason's office. As usual he didn't bother to knock but turned the handle and walked in.

'Don't think your daughter cares for me', he said with a sly grin as he helped himself to a chair.

'That's a monumental understatement', Jason observed dryly. 'The truth is you're far from being everyone's cup of tea.'

'No, but I have my uses, don't I?'

Jason ignored the question.

'Well, how did it go?' he asked.

'On the whole it was a very satisfactory visit. You should have seen old Playford's face when he walked into his office and found me sitting there.'

'How did you find the other one?'

'The Yard bloke? He's not as wooden as *our* Sherlock Holmes.

He asked the hell of a lot of questions; all routine ones. I should think he's a good plodder.'

'I shouldn't underestimate him', Jason said lighting another cigarette from the butt of the one he had just finished. Gazing at Prentice with a shrewd expression, he went on, 'I fear you've already played somewhat into their hands by looking so blasted pleased with yourself. I warned you about it too.'

'Oh, stuff it, Gus. I *am* pleased with myself. Haven't I good reason to be? Things couldn't have worked out better.'

It was very clear that Jason didn't approve of his visitor's cheerful spirits and he now stared at him with a marked degree of cool contempt. Prentice shifted uncomfortably in his chair and said with studied indifference:

'I imagine they'll be on to you soon to corroborate what I told them.'

'Did you *volunteer* the information or did they ask you where you were at the time of the murder?'

'The latter.'

'Thank heavens, at least, that you didn't burst out with that unasked.'

Prentice flushed angrily but said nothing. There was no gain in losing his temper with Jason at this juncture.

For a time silence reigned while Jason squinted at the top of his freshly-lit cigarette. Then he said:

'Potts was along here this morning.'

'I know; you said so on the phone. What did he want?'

Jason slowly moistened his lips with the tip of his tongue and fixed Prentice with a cold catlike gaze whose chilling aloofness invariably disconcerted those upon whom it was turned. It was always as though he was about to impart a few inadequate words on the art of swimming before dispassionately toppling his victim head-first into unfathomable depths.

'I'll tell you what he told myself and the police,' he said, watching Prentice as a cat might a cornered mouse, 'and you can then draw your own conclusions.'

An old reporter on one of the family papers had once told Dominic that whenever he was hard-up for a story he went along to the courts. It mattered little, he had said, which court: civil, criminal, divorce, each was as good as the other providing enough raw material to fill a whole newspaper. There was nowhere better, according to him, for surveying human nature beneath a microscope and any young reporter who could spend half an hour in a court without finding something to write about ought to turn to hedge-clipping. For some reason he seemed to regard this as the most imaginative of all occupations and it was the one to which he was wont to consign anyone whom he considered useless at his own job. Over a long period of years there were few from Prime Ministers down who he hadn't opined would be more profitably thus occupied.

It would, however, be untrue to pretend that it was this piece of advice which primarily led Dominic into Wenley Magistrates' Court on this particular morning, though it probably played its contributory part deep down in his sub-conscious. All he was aware of was the desire to get out of the biting northeast wind and kill three-quarters of an hour as cheaply as possible. He was due to meet Claudia for lunch a few minutes before one and till then a visit to court seemed best to meet his requirements. It would be warm, it was free, it was close by and it might also be sufficiently diverting to lift his mind off his present troubles. Almost overwhelming troubles they had seemed recently.

He tiptoed in and found an inconspicuous place in the back row of the tiered seats behind the dock, whose glossy-headed occupant resembled from the rear an advertisement for a popular hair-cream. Dominic turned his attention to the witness-box and guessed in a moment that the solid frame that filled it belonged to a police officer.

'I cautioned the defendant', the witness was saying when Mr. Quench, the clerk, who was surreptitiously doing *The Times* crossword looked up and said sharply:

'What did you actually say to him?'

The officer drew a breath and recited:

'I told him that he was not obliged to say anything unless he wished to do so, but that anything he did say would be taken down in writing and might be given in evidence at his trial.'

Mr. Quench nodded.

'All right, go on', he said, returning to his crossword, oblivious of the humouring look bestowed upon him. The officer took another breath and resumed his set course.

'After I had cautioned the defendant, I told him that I had reason to believe he had in his possession two hundred and fifty-two pairs of Mark IV non-lined industrial gloves which had been unlawfully removed from the premises of Messrs. Hardpick of Fireling Street, Wenley. I then cautioned him and he said, "There's more than that".'

As Dominic became more accustomed to his surroundings, he noticed that the officer was giving his evidence at dictation speed and that it was being written down by one of the assistant clerks. Mr. Quench, who sat beside his assistant, was, as already stated, doing *The Times* crossword and the two presiding Justices, of whom one was Potts, wore glazed expressions of boredom.

'. . . as soon as the defendant said that I immediately cautioned him', the officer continued like a heavy galleon under steady sail and the assistant clerk's pen slid automatically over the paper. It was a stage which is frequently reached in cases where an accused has to be committed to stand trial at Assizes or Quarter Sessions. Every word of every witness has to be recorded in the form of a deposition and often by the time a police officer reaches the box, it is apparent that a *prima facie* case has already been established (that is, sufficient evidence adduced to justify the committal for trial). There was therefore some excuse for the generally torpid atmosphere and the assistant clerk and the officer would have been undoubtedly happier if they could have enacted their parts in more congenial surroundings, since no one in court appeared to pay them the slightest interest. Alas, the rules are not that liberal and the law though sometimes falling short of majesty is never familiar.

The officer's evidence droned on. 'The defendant then said to me, "have you found the firemen's boots as well?' I at once cautioned him and he continued, "They are in the cupboard beneath the stairs. I got them the same time as the gloves. I thought they was a job lot and I wouldn't have touched them if I'd know they was hot." I asked the defendant if he cared to tell me how much he had paid for them. I cautioned him and he replied. . . .'

It was perhaps not surprising that Dominic's thoughts wandered to matters a good deal more relevant to his own existence. He had realized for some time that his almost daily visits to Wenley (about thirty miles from where he lived in the neighbouring county) could not continue indefinitely. Sooner or later his father would find out that his absences from the branch newspaper office where he was supposed to be learning the business were more marked than his attendances. The only reason it hadn't already come to his notice was because as High Sheriff of the County Sir Gilbert Trevane had for the past ten days been heavily engaged waiting upon Her Majesty's Judges of Assize. It should perhaps be explained that he also owned a chain of provincial newspapers, was an ex-M.P. and a very dominant personality and that Dominic had finally succumbed to a mixture of paternal blandishments and threats in agreeing to enter the family business, though it was a prospect that held small joy for him.

How soon and how near he had come to the brink of disaster was now vividly evoked in his mind, for it was here in Wenley Magistrates' Court that it had all begun. He shuddered at the thought of what his father's reaction would have been if he had learnt the truth. It had been a close shave, and heaven knew danger still encompassed him – danger even greater than he suspected.

Meanwhile the officer continued to intone his evidence.

'I next cautioned the defendant and said to him. . . .'

Dominic's mind switched back to the day he had rushed to Jason in his panic, for it was also on that fateful visit that he had met Claudia for the first time and immediately fallen in love with her. It was not this, however, which was causing him now to lose sleep. It was the subsequent nightmarish incident whose proportions had recently and terrifyingly increased. How long he could go on keeping it all to himself, he dared not guess. The urge to discuss it with someone, with Claudia in particular, was at times overwhelming; but the dangers were so appalling that he more often than not felt it was a secret which must go with him to the grave – that is if he was lucky enough. As these thoughts stampeded around his head, he gnawed viciously at his thumbnail, a habit unknown to him but a week before.

The officer's evidence was at last nearing an end.

'I then cautioned and charged the defendant with the offences in respect of which he now appears before the Court and he made no reply.' He turned towards Potts on the Bench and said complacently, 'That is my evidence, your worships.'

Mr. Quench immediately seized the deposition from his assistant and read it out at breakneck speed, while from time to time making small pencilled strokes on his blotter. When he had finished he consulted the tally and with one eyebrow mildly cocked said:

'Officer, did you really caution the defendant seven times?'

The officer's expression at once became stonily blank and staring straight to his fore like a Guardsman on parade, he replied:

'My evidence is as I've given it, sir.'

'Very well, I just thought I'd ask. It seemed a little excessive in an interview that I gather lasted less than a quarter of an hour, but so be it. It's your evidence, not mine.'

His tone was offensively sarcastic, but Potts, who had not been listening to the evidence, missed this short interchange. Like Dominic, he had encouraged his mind to wander elsewhere. The predominant emotion which welled up within him and tinged all his thoughts was self-pity. Why did such things have to happen to him? Why did he have to have an unfaithful wife whose caperings had threatened all his highest hopes and ambitions? But of more pressing importance, would the steps he had taken be sufficient to restore matrimonial law and order within his home? And what would he do if, despite all, he was suddenly engulfed by a floodtide of local newspaper rumour and gossip? It was all damnable and hideously unfair. Cold rage against his wife surged through his body as he pondered the situation. It was she and she alone who was responsible.

Now that Notley was dead, he no longer had any feelings about him and in any event it had fundamentally always been Eileen's fault. It was she who had caused him to take ruthless measures; to concoct and fabricate and adopt false positions; and even now, he realized, he couldn't be sure he knew the whole truth. Eileen was indeed a deep one – a dangerously deep one. And now, thinking back over the past few days, he decided it was odd the way she had reacted to her ex-lover's death. She had displayed neither relief nor sorrow – not in his presence anyway, but you could never tell with her. It suddenly came to Potts that if she could regard a lover's demise with such equanimity, how would she react to an expendable husband's – to his, in fact? Eileen had already shown she didn't *need* him: Supposing she didn't *want* him either? He shivered.

This line of torturing thought was fortunately interrupted by Mr. Quench, who looked round from his seat below and said:

'Will you now formally commit the defendant to the next Quarter Sessions?'

Potts looked at the figure standing in the dock and shook himself back to reality.

'Joshua Philby', he said with judicial solemnity, glancing at the court register in front of him.

'No, no', Mr. Quench broke in crossly. 'It's the next name down. It's, it's. . . .' Feverishly he hunted amongst the papers which littered his own desk, finally pouncing on the day's court list. 'It's Cecil Hindercup – number six in your register.'

'Cecil Hindercup', Potts began again. 'We have listened with great care to all the evidence which has been given before us and we find that a *prima facie* case has been established. You will therefore be committed to take your trial at the next Wenley Borough Quarter Sessions.'

While he was speaking, Mr. Quench's face registered increasing exasperation, since the first part of Potts's oration, if required at all, should have come before he, the clerk, had meaninglessly intoned the long legal formula known as The Statutory Caution. In answer to this, the defendant, having already admitted everything several times over to the police, had replied, 'I plead not guilty and reserve my defence.' Thereafter Potts's last few words were all that were either needed or appropriate.

However it was now all over. The defendant disappeared out of sight down the dock stairs, the spectators wandered out, Mr. Quench hurried away to his lunch with no thought for aught else, and Potts and his fellow Justice slipped unobtrusively out of the door labelled MAGISTRATES ONLY.

As Dominic strode along to the small café where he and Claudia met for their three-course three-and-sixpenny lunch, he found himself vaguely haunted by something which had happened while he'd been in court: something so fleeting that it had left on his conscious mind no stronger impression that a money-spider would on an elephant's back. He found it nevertheless irking that it refused to be summoned up from the mysterious depths where it had gone to ground.

CHAPTER TWELVE

AT one o'clock Detective-Inspector Playford joined the general pilgrimage in search of food. It required something more urgent than a murder investigation to cause him willingly to forego his journey home for the ample but starchy lunch prepared by Mrs. Playford. Some sort of stew with potatoes, dumplings and large slices of bread to mop up the rich gravy had become his standard fuel and the one on which he ran best. 'Sensible food' was what he called it.

Manton, for his part, had decided against returning to the hotel for lunch and had ordered coffee and sandwiches to be sent up to the office. He wanted to discuss the case with Talper who, however, didn't arrive back till he had finished his food and was beoming restive. Playford would have unhesitatingly attributed this to not having a proper hot meal, but Manton knew it was a sign of dissatisfaction with the progress of his investigation.

Once it had been established that Notley was the murder victim, Prentice had naturally become prime suspect. But before they had ever had time fully to mobilize their thoughts against him, he had walked in, sprung an alibi and walked out again. Though he had not yet had an opportunity of checking the alibi, Manton had no doubt that Jason would support it, since Prentice would never have dared involve him without first being sure of his ground. If it was a false alibi, it wouldn't be broken at the Jason link; of that Manton was quite certain.

While he was thus frowningly engaged, the door opened and Sergeant Talper came in. Soon Manton felt his sense of nervous irritation begin to dissolve. There was something timeless and soothing about his sergeant's unruffled presence which never failed to help restore his own sense of perspective.

'There's your lunch, Andy', he said, nodding at the tray on the desk. 'You eat and I'll tell you the morning's developments. Then you can give me an account of your activities.'

By the time Manton had finished, Talper had polished off

the sandwiches, drunk the last dregs of the coffee and got his pipe well alight.

'Now it's your turn', Manton said.

Talper took the pipe from his mouth, surveyed it lovingly from stem to bowl, and replaced it.

'I've found out, sir, that Notley and Miss Jason dined together on the night of his death and that they had a bit of a row on the pavement outside the hotel when they were leaving. The night porter who had just come on duty, witnessed it.' He went on to retail a somewhat lurid version of the face-slapping incident and when he had finished, Manton said:

'That can only have been about half an hour before his death. We must see Miss Jason about it. I don't suppose for a moment that she murdered him, but. . . .'

'But she had a motive and could have', Talper said, finishing the sentence for him.

'Mmm, we want to know what the row was about and what she did afterwards. She may well have been the last person to have seen him alive.'

'I wasn't able to find anyone who'd seen either of them after they'd parted company outside the hotel.'

'We may be able to do something about that when we know her story. It'll be a question of trying to find independent corroboration of what she tells us about her movements. What else have you unearthed?'

'I went along to the telephone exchange as you suggested, sir.'

'I can guess,' Manton said resignedly and went on, 'The automatic telephone may be one of science's less dangerous developments but it still doesn't help unfortunate detectives who would sometimes dearly like to be able to trace a call.'

'Well, it so happens that we're in luck for once', Talper said, happy to be the bearer of better news. 'I found the operator who was on duty the evening before last – a chap called Wicks – and he remembers someone trying to get through to Potts's number. He can't recall the exact time but he knows it was around half past nine because he had just opened his thermos flask of cocoa which he brings on evening duty with him and he says he always does that as soon after half past nine as he can.'

'Yes, but what does he remember?' Manton asked, impatiently brushing aside the circumstantial detail.

'That someone from a call-box got through to him and said he'd been talking to Wenley 5684 – that's Potts's number – and had been cut off. He told the operator that he had tried to get through again but there was no reply, and he wanted the exchange to have a go.'

'Did they?'

'Yes, the operator then rang the number but there was still

no reply. He told the caller he couldn't get any answer and the caller hung up.'

'Did he know where the call was coming from? Don't you have to give your number when you're speaking from a public box?'

'Yes, he remembered that too because it was rather a distinctive number. It was 222211. I've since checked and found it belongs to a public telephone box which stands at a road junction about two hundred yards from Notley's Garage.'

'Has he any clue which would help us to trace the caller?'

'No. It was a man: that's all he can say.'

'An excited man? an incoherent man? a calm man? a deep-voiced man?' Manton asked hopefully.

'Just an ordinary man', Talper replied. 'I'm afraid he can't remember anything special about him. One wouldn't really expect him to.'

'But why does he remember the incident at all?' Manton asked with slight suspicion. 'After all, quite a few people must get through to the exchange on similar quests. What was there to impress the detail of this one on *his* mind?'

'I particularly asked him that. Apparently this caller engaged him in a certain amount of chit-chat while he was trying to get through to Potts's number; said he knew there was someone there and he suspected they might be deliberately not answering. He told the operator to give a good long ring.'

'I see', Manton said and added, 'So much for Potts's mysterious caller. At least we seem to have confirmed his existence.'

Most of the afternoon, Manton spent conferring with the pathologist who had completed his autopsy on Notley's body and with the scientific officer from the Home Office Forensic Science Laboratory who had made a full examination of the car and of Notley's burnt-out office.

Dr. Nation, the pathologist, was a small birdlike man whose impeccable dress looked more appropriate to a City business house than the chain of mortuaries which marked his daily course. He greeted Manton with simple brevity.

'Cause of death, asphyxia', he said in clipped tones. 'That's what you want to know, isn't it?'

'Yes, sir. Nothing special otherwise?'

'I don't know what you mean by "otherwise" and as to "nothing special", each autopsy I perform is "special" to me and it's certainly a unique experience for the corpse – even though he is past taking any interest in it.'

'I meant was it a *straightforward* case of asphyxia?' Manton said.

'In my view, yes. I know what's in your mind; you're wondering whether he might not have been stunned or involved in some violence before being incinerated?' Manton nodded and the pathologist went on, 'Seeing the extent to which the body was burnt, particularly the head, I can't answer that with a hundred per cent certainty but I can say that it appeared to be a straight-forward case of asphyxia by suffocation without any supple-mentary complications. If he had, say, been knocked unconscious before his office was set alight, I might, despite the degree of burning, have found signs of it.' He reached for his bowler hat, gloves and umbrella which lay on a table in the mortuary office and said, 'Anything else you want to know before I go?'

'No, thank you, sir. At least, nothing that can't wait till I've read your full report.'

'Ah!' Dr. Nation replied with a sudden gleam in his eye. 'And how soon do you want that?' Quickly he added, 'It's no good your saying by this evening, because you won't get it. I'll try and let you have it within forty-eight hours.'

'That should be all right', Manton agreed cautiously.

'Of course it will. I've told you all you need to know for the time being and I promise you I've got nothing up my sleeve which will in any way help you to find the murderer.'

On this matter-of-fact note, he departed.

Manton's interview with Mr. Jameson of the laboratory was quite different, though he learnt very little which either helped him or which he hadn't already guessed. Mr. Jameson, a frail and youthful person of a type to excite anyone with mothering instincts, merely succeeded in confirming what he already sup-posed: namely that the fire in Notley's office had started by petrol being poured beneath the door and becoming ignited by the small bowl-type electric fire which stood just inside: and that the charge beneath the driver's seat in the car had been wired to be operated by the indicator switch on the steering-column.

'The one method was as ingenious as the other was crude', said Mr. Jameson with a wan smile.

'Yes,' Manton replied, 'which means that if both were the work of the same person, he had ample time for the one but was compelled to do a rush job on the other.'

'That's rather clever', Mr. Jameson said admiringly. 'Your reasoning, I mean. I note you say "he". You think then, it's a man you're looking for?'

'Isn't it more likely? I'm not saying a woman *couldn't* have fixed the car but it's much more a man's job. The other could have been equally well done by a woman, however, and in some ways bears the marks of being a feminine crime. The indirectness of it, for example; the avoiding being in at the actual kill, if you follow me.'

Mr. Jameson nodded and said:

'Yes, women usually prefer not to witness their victims' death agonies. There have, of course, been some notable exceptions. But what you say also applies to the attempt to blow Prentice up.'

'A disinclination to be present at the kill, you mean?'

Mr. Jameson nodded again and a lock of curly hair fell across his forehead.

'But I think there were quite different considerations in that case', Manton went on. 'Prentice, one is driven to assume, had to be killed without delay as soon as he was released from prison, and before ever he had an opportunity of contacting anyone in the outside world. The car idea was highly ingenious and very nearly achieved this.'

'It'll be interesting to look back later on and see how close to the truth your present reasoning is', Mr. Jameson said with something almost approaching enthusiasm.

Manton looked at him sardonically and said:

'I'll leave you to do that for me. Once I've got someone arrested, I'm not much interested in intellectual post-mortem games. The art is being able to recognize facts for what they are, because as you know false deductions can be very costly in criminal investigations.'

He bade Mr. Jameson farewell with an exhortation to let him have a full written report as early as possible. On his return to headquarters, Manton found Inspector Playford fulminating alone in his room.

'Look at this', he said menacingly, thrusting a copy of the *Wenley Evening Post* into Manton's hands. 'Of all the something sauce. . . .'

On the front page was a flattering photograph of Julian Prentice taken many years before and above it a large black headline which read:

PRENTICE SENSATION
'POLICE NOW PERFECTLY SATISFIED I HAD NOTHING TO DO WITH NOTLEY'S DEATH', PRENTICE SAYS.

JULIAN PRENTICE, 42-YEAR-OLD RESIDENT OF WENLEY WHO MYSTERIOUSLY DISAPPEARED FROM HOSPITAL LAST WEDNESDAY AFTER AN ATTEMPT HAD BEEN MADE ON HIS LIFE, MADE A SENSATIONAL REAPPEARANCE IN THE TOWN TO-DAY. AFTER VISITING POLICE HEADQUARTERS THIS MORNING HE SPOKE TO YOUR REPORTER AND FRANKLY ANSWERED QUESTIONS ABOUT HIMSELF.

'I HAD EVERY REASON TO BELIEVE MY LIFE MIGHT STILL BE

IN DANGER AND THAT I WASN'T AT ALL SAFE IN HOSPITAL', HE TOLD ME WITH A SMILE. 'HENCE MY DECISION TO DISAPPEAR.'

MR. PRENTICE DECLINED TO SAY WHERE HE HAD BEEN BUT INSISTED THERE WAS NO MYSTERY ABOUT IT OTHER THAN HIS WISH TO SAVE EMBARRASSMENT TO CERTAIN PEOPLE. HE WENT ON, 'AS SOON AS I LEARNT OF MR. NOTLEY'S DEATH, I CONCEIVED IT MY DUTY TO GO AND SEE IF I COULD HELP THE POLICE. I HAVE JUST COME FROM THEM NOW.'

IT IS GATHERED THAT MR. PRENTICE WAS ASKED A LARGE NUMBER OF QUESTIONS, AS A RESULT OF WHICH THE POLICE ARE NOW ENTIRELY SATISFIED ABOUT HIS MOVEMENTS ON THE EVENING OF THE ALLEGED CRIME. 'IT WAS A FRANK AND FRIENDLY EXCHANGE OF INFORMATION,' MR. PRENTICE CONCLUDED, 'AND THEY NOW KNOW I WAS WITH FRIENDS AT THE TIME OF MR. NOTLEY'S SUPPOSED MURDER.'

The report finished with a colourful résumé of events leading up to the present position and reminded its readers that the two experienced Scotland Yard officers who had been called in were still actively engaged in their inquiries and that spectacular developments could be hourly expected.

'Spectacular developments indeed', Manton said with a grunt. 'I wish there were some.'

'But what about all he's said: have you ever read such a slab of impudent lies?'

'Mmm', Manton murmured thoughtfully. 'In the circumstances, I think we'd better go and see Jason and find out precisely what he has to say about Prentice's alibi. It's also time we saw Claudia Jason.' He looked at his watch. 'They should both be at home now; it's after seven and we can kill the two birds at once – possibly even a third as well.' Playford looked blank and Manton explained, 'Prentice, the guest these last few days of Augustus Jason.'

CHAPTER THIRTEEN

AT Manton's direction the car was parked a discreet distance from Jason's house and he and Playford walked the remainder of the way. The deserted, poorly-lit road, flanked by large, stone houses which stood respectfully back in their overgrown gardens, provided an atmosphere of weary melancholy.

In silence they walked up the drive which was thickly-carpeted with sodden leaves. A dim yellow reflection which came through the glass panel above the front door was the only sign of life. Manton stood back and gazed up at the front of the building, while Playford first pressed the bell and then vigorously attacked the door with the heavy knocker.

It was Claudia who eventually opened it, giving a little gasp when she saw who were her visitors.

'Oh, it's you', she said.

'Good evening, Miss Jason', Manton said affably, stepping forward. 'Is your father in?'

'No, he's not back yet. He . . . er . . . he had a late appointment.'

'No matter. We'd also like to have a word with *you*. So may we come in? Probably by the time we've finished your father will be back.'

For a while Claudia stood in the doorway staring uncertainly from one to the other of them. There was no doubt that she was attractive. She radiated feminine appeal as she studied them with grey-green eyes which were calm but grave. Her trim and cool self-assurance were exemplified in her present expression and her mouth was small and deliciously red. She seemed, however, to have no wish to open it. Finally she stood aside and said:

'All right.'

Manton stepped forward and punctiliously wiped his shoes before entering. Indeed, he did it so thoroughly that Playford thought he displayed unnecessary respect, not realizing it was a mere expedient for examining his surroundings at greater leisure.

Manton's first impression was that the interior of the house was in perfect keeping with the outside. The hall, which was square, was filled with several huge pieces of solid mahogany furniture which would have gone clean through the floor of any modern house. There was also an arresting odour about the place which could have been compounded of everything from boiled cabbage to the dry mustiness of a catacomb.

Claudia led the way across to a door at the far side. It was the left-hand one of two and she opened it and went in to what was clearly the drawing-room. The high ceiling was yellow with dirt, the wallpaper was faded (though with possible improvement to its pattern) and the carpet had seen better days. There were two large china cabinets against the walls, each full of bric-à-brac collected over three generations. The various pieces, which had once been purchased with a high appreciation of their worth, now had no more individuality than cherries in a pie. The mantelpiece was also laden with small assorted ornaments which flanked an enormous black marble clock of monstrous baroque design whose hands had long been locked at five past one.

'Won't you sit down', Claudia said without enthusiasm, as she perched herself on the arm of a chair.

Manton and Playford accepted the invitation and sank back together on the capacious sofa. Too late Manton realized their error. In his view two police officers reclining side by side as they were could hardly fail to appear comic. He eased himself gently forward, leaving Inspector Playford lolling inelegantly like one who has obviously fed too well.

'I believe you saw Notley on the evening of his death, Miss Jason?' he began, coming to the point without delay.

'Yes, I had dinner with him.'

'Was that at his invitation?'

'Yes. If you want to know, he asked me out to dinner several times.'

'Were you fond of him?'

'He could be quite amusing', she said slowly and then made a slight face suggesting distaste. 'But I didn't have any special feelings toward him.'

'You weren't in love with him?'

'Good heavens, no. What on earth makes you think that?'

'I don't. I'm simply a seeker after information', Manton said disarmingly.

'Well, I wasn't. Quite frankly I didn't even like him, let alone love him.'

'But you accepted his invitations out to dinner?'

Claudia flushed.

'As I've already told you, he could be amusing company; but I don't have to love every man who takes me out to dinner.' Her tone clearly indicated that the question had piqued her and after a brief pause, she said with careful emphasis, 'He *amused* me and he *interested* me. Now are you satisfied?'

'Oh perfectly', said Manton with a bland smile. 'I'm only sorry you found the question such an embarrassing one.'

She seemed on the point of a further rejoinder, but restrained herself.

'What time did you part company that evening?'

'Soon after nine.'

'Where?'

'Outside the hotel. We had a row. He wanted me to go back to his flat with him and I refused. He was a bit tight and became truculent.'

So far the truth, Manton thought, watching her with his bright blue eyes. What may soon be discovered is whether it comes naturally or from expediency. She's obviously tumbled to the fact that if we don't already know all about her movements that night, there's nothing she can now do to conceal them.

'What happened after the row?' he asked.

91

'I slapped his face and left him', she replied.

'Did you see him again after that?'

'No.'

'You didn't see where he went or what he did?'

'N-no, I didn't.'

'And what did you do?'

'I came straight home.'

'Did you go near his garage on your way back?'

'I passed it.'

'You passed it?' Manton said with interest.

'Yes, have you any objection?'

She's certainly an independent young miss, he mused: She's also a trifle prickly on certain subjects.

'Do you know whether Notley was there when you passed?'

'How should I? I didn't go in.'

'You might have seen his car outside.'

'I didn't.'

'Do you mean it wasn't there or you didn't look?'

'The latter. I walked straight past and didn't stop.'

'You didn't happen to notice any lights on in the garage?'

'I've told you, I saw nothing. You seem to think I sauntered by like a window-gazer. I can promise you I wasn't in that sort of mood after what had happened.'

Though Manton was generally regarded as being a very fair officer, this didn't mean that he pursued his inquiries without vigour and determination. Now, however, he suddenly felt inhibited about the questions he was proposing to ask concerning Prentice's recent movements. It was tackling Jason through his daughter and though he didn't bother to analyse his feeling, deep down he knew that he would have it on his conscience if he did so. He had a vague idea that things were already difficult enough for Claudia without his making them more so by his opportunism. So, switching the subject abruptly, he asked:

'Did you have many clients to see you at the office this morning, Miss Jason?'

She stared at him suspiciously before answering.

'Two', she said cautiously.

'Will you tell me who they were?'

'I don't think you have any right to ask that, but I will tell you, just to prevent my refusal becoming an outsize red herring. They were a Mrs. Shepherd and a Miss Young in that order.'

'You didn't have any male visitors?' he said with dewy innocence.

Claudia hesitated a second.

'You said "clients", Superintendent', she said carefully, as though afraid the words might break in her mouth.

'Because I didn't think a busy solicitor saw anyone other than clients in office hours.'

A silence ensued which was eventually broken by Manton.

'Well, Miss Jason?'

'A friend did call in for a few minutes', she said slowly.

'A male friend?'

She nodded.

'May I ask his name?'

'And may *I* ask why you want it?' This time there was no mistaking the note of defiance in her tone and she went on, 'I've already answered a very great number of questions, but I am not prepared to do so any more unless you can first satisfy me about your reasons for asking them.'

Inspector Playford heaved himself forward at this note of crisis but Manton merely gave Claudia a wry smile and said nothing. The truth was, that he'd been expecting it for some time and was only surprised that she had been amenable for so long.

Suddenly there was a movement over by the door and Augustus Jason's soft tones came out of the shadows.

'I thought I saw the imprints of big heavy boots in the hall.' He came across to where they were sitting and looking down at Playford said, 'I should have expected you, Herbert, to have told your colleague that I don't like being visited by the police at my home. I regard it as an unnecessary intrusion of my privacy.'

'The visit is my responsibility', Manton said, quickly standing up.

'I don't doubt it, but unless you have either a warrant for my arrest or one to search my house, I'd be glad if you would now take your leave.'

'You know quite well that we have neither and that we shouldn't be here if your daughter hadn't invited us in.'

'We'll let that rather naive remark pass, shall we? Well, what is the urgent business that has brought you?'

Manton looked meaningly from father to daughter and Jason said:

'You'd better leave us, sweetie. I'll be ready for my supper in a few minutes.'

Claudia turned and left the room without further comment. When the door had closed behind her, Manton said:

'Will you tell us your movements on the evening of Notley's death, Mr. Jason?'

He had decided that a frontal assault was in this instance the best method of approach, though he had little doubt that Jason would contrive to turn it.

'Do you suspect me of having murdered him?' Jason countered and then murmured, 'But no, you obviously won't answer that and it remains for me to decide whether or not to answer *your* question.'

93

Playford started to expostulate but Manton quickly motioned him to stay silent. The incident was not, however, lost on Jason and he bestowed a sour smile on each of them.

'I was at home the whole evening', he said, darting his gaze from one to the other as if to register their minutest reaction.

'Were you alone?'

'No, as you already know, Prentice was with me – for part of the time.'

Manton suddenly felt a tingle of excitement. He knew Jason had intended this and been quick to notice it. The point was whether it was just another sly game or whether this time he was about to give a genuine lead.

Jason for his part clearly wanted to be primed by further questions, it being part of his conversation technique to lead people by a ring through the nose. On this occasion Manton was prepared to be ringed and led.

'As far as you can recollect, when did Prentice arrive and depart?' he asked.

'He left at about twenty minutes past nine.'

'Are you sure of that? You see he told us he was in your company the whole evening.'

'I know he did, but I'm afraid he wasn't.'

'Any idea why he should lie about it?'

'That's not a question for this witness to answer', Jason replied smoothly.

'Where was he going?'

'He had an appointment, but I don't know where or with whom.'

There was a long silence, at the end of which Manton said:

'What it amounts to is that you don't support his alibi for the time when Notley was murdered?'

'I'm neither interested in supporting his alibi nor in refuting it. I've given you the truth and what anyone else has told you is their concern.'

'How long would it take to get from here to Notley's Garage?' Manton asked, turning to Playford, who puckered his lips as he did some mental arithmetic.

'It's about a ten-minute walk across the recreation ground and almost as long to go round by car.'

Manton switched back to Jason who had taken up a position in front of the fireplace.

'Were you alone in the house after Prentice left you?'

'I was.'

'Where was your daughter?'

For one fraction of a split second, Jason looked put out. It was as if a tiny crack in his armour had been laid bare.

'She came in very shortly after Prentice had gone,' he said

quickly and added, 'it can't have been more than a few minutes after.'

'Five for example?' Manton asked.

'Much less. Three at the most.'

'Then the odds are that they must have passed each other quite close to the house?' Manton pressed.

Jason shrugged his shoulders impatiently.

'How should I know?' It was a particularly dark night and it's perfectly reasonable they wouldn't have seen each other, even if they did pass.'

'So you do know that they didn't see one another?'

'Look, Mr. Superintendent, don't start trying to trick me with your clever questions', Jason said with angry sarcasm.

Manton decided to let the matter rest and turned to Playford who showed signs of wanting to speak.

'In answer to one of Mr. Manton's earlier questions, you said what time Prentice left here; but you were also asked what time he'd arrived and that you haven't yet told us.'

'He had arrived about half past two.'

'Nearly seven hours before?'

'Two days and seven hours', Jason said with a jeering smile.

Playford seemed to regard the admission as one of crucial importance.

'You realize what you're telling us?'

'I do indeed.'

'Namely that you harboured Prentice on his escape from hospital?'

Turning to Manton, Jason said:

'Now you know what I'm up against in this town. Because someone leaves hospital – as he has every right to do – and comes to spend a few days in my house – which is not yet a contravention of the law – it's said that he "escaped" and that I have "harboured" him. It just goes to prove how a vivid imagination, allied to a spate of wishful thinking, can distort a few simple, innocent facts.' He looked back at Playford and continued, "If you weren't shortly due to retire, Herbert, I should have to consider seeking official protection from such wicked prejudice. Luckily I'm too fond of you to want to take such drastic action when you're so near to going – even though it might provide a good final chapter to your memoirs.'

Playford snorted, plainly, scornfully and angrily.

'Is Prentice still here?' Manton asked, abruptly.

'No, he departed suddenly this afternoon.'

'So he has disappeared again, eh?' Manton said softly. There was something in his tone and Jason's reaction to it that produced a fleeting moment of almost palpable tension. Then without a word Jason walked suddenly across to the door, opened it and ostentatiously waited for the two men to take their leave.

A few moments later they were walking back down the drive while a watery moon and high scudding clouds contrived with the gently twitching branches of two great beech trees to encompass them with strange and mysterious shapes.

'He'd just come from seeing Potts', Playford said when they were almost at the gate.

'Oh, how do you know that?' Manton asked in surprise.

'He had traces of orange-yellow sand on the toe-cap of one of his shoes and the Potts's drive is the only place it could have come from.'

'I say, that's real detection', Manton said with genuine admiration.

They arrived back at headquarters to find Talper alone in Inspector Playford's office poring over the documents which they had earlier removed from Notley's safe.

'Found anything?' Manton asked as he hung up his hat and coat.

'Yes, sir. Notley was financially in the gutter.' Sergeant Talper paused to let this dramatic piece of news sink in and then went on, 'He had a vast overdraft, his garage business was mortgaged to the last pint of petrol and he had a number of large outstanding debts – not least to the revenue authorities.'

'So he was a man of straw, eh?' Manton said, his eyes bright with interest. 'How did you find all this out?'

'I made a few discreet inquiries at his bank. Nothing official of course.'

Manton nodded understandingly.

'About how much did he owe?'

'Something in the region of ten thousand pounds.'

'Did he now! That's very interesting. To what extent it bears on his murder we've yet to find out, though it clearly provides a few more motives all round.' He bit gently at a fingernail and said, 'What about that correspondence between him and Jason? Anything further there?'

'Some of the letters seem to hint at some shady deals – tax evasion and that sort of thing, but there's nothing obviously connected with the murder.'

'But one can safely assume that Jason knew of his financial position', Manton said in thoughtful comment and lapsed into silence.

After further short discussion, Playford excused himself and departed to intensify the search for Prentice. Orders were brief and to the point. He was to be found and brought to headquarters without delay.

'Think we've got enough on which to charge him?' Talper asked when Manton had apprised him of their visit to Jason.

'I'm not sure, but we certainly shall have if he gives way at all on his alibi.'

'It's queer the way he boasted of his alibi; even dished it out in great spoonfuls to the Press, and now Jason doesn't support it.'

'I know. What's more, when he came here this morning, I'm certain the whole object of his visit was to throw it in our faces. He was absolutely cockahoop and it follows he can't have had an inkling that within a few hours Jason would sell him down the river.'

'And that means,' Talper broke in, 'either that Jason is deliberately lying and giving him a good push, head-first into the noose, or that Jason has had some quick second thoughts about supporting an alibi which he knows to be false. If so, what *are* his thoughts and why did he agree to support it in the first place?'

'It might be either. I certainly wouldn't put it past Jason to swear someone's life away in sufficiently cogent circumstances. For example in order to protect himself – or his daughter. Nevertheless I think it's more likely that the alibi is false and that Jason, having originally agreed to support it, has had, as you say, some very smart second thoughts on the subject.'

'It would be nice to see Prentice's face when he hears of Jason's duplicity.'

'It would indeed,' Manton agreed heartily. He idly picked up a small pocket diary from the desk. It was the one which had been found in Notley's safe.

'I suppose you haven't deciphered any of this, have you, Andy?'

Talper put out a hand for it and turned to the page at the back on which appeared the rough sketch of a road junction. He bent it open and placed it flat on the desk.

'Know what I think that is, sir?' he asked.

Manton shook his head.

'A plan of the road in the vicinity of Potts's house. If you remember, there is a junction about a hundred and fifty yards from his place.'

'Y-yes,' Manton said slowly, 'but isn't it rather a long shot to . . .'

'Look, sir,' Sergeant Talper interrupted. 'The dot clearly indicates a house and surely the number above it – the twelve – must refer to the particular one.'

'Yes, Andy, you're right and Potts's house *is* number twelve', Manton said excitedly while Talper purred with satisfaction.

'But what do these other two figures refer to? A hundred and sixty-five and seventy?'

'I've no idea', Talper said flatly.

'They're most likely to be distances in feet or yards, aren't they?' Manton went on, thinking aloud.

'They could be, sir.'

'Surely it's more than "could" – that is if they're related at all to the sketch and they certainly seem to be. What about this? You said just now that Potts's house is about a hundred and fifty yards from the road junction: supposing it's exactly a hundred and sixty-five.'

Talper nodded with enthusiasm.

'I'll go and pace it out myself, sir,' he said.

'And if it is, what's it all amount to?' Manton said in a puzzled tone. 'Why should Notley have a sketch of the area of Potts's home in his diary?'

'And those times and the other figures for January and February, what on earth do they mean?' added Talper like a dejected Greek chorus.

Suddenly Manton seized the diary and turned back to the page for the week in March where there appeared a time recorded on each of five consecutive days. He stared at it with furrowed brow and then said dreamily:

'I wonder ... yes, I wonder if this diary mayn't be the link between two seemingly unconnected events?'

CHAPTER FOURTEEN

THE next morning at a quarter to ten, the Chief Constable presided over a conference attended by Manton, Playford and Talper.

Outside, Wenley lay enveloped in its first real fog of the autumn and Playford found himself staring with vacant gloom out of the window at the dismal prospect.

Despite the fact that several officers of the C.I.D. had spent cold, disturbed nights, Prentice had not been found and this failure clearly piqued the Chief, who seemed to regard it as proof of their not having tried hard enough.

'He's *got* to be found', he said energetically, as though strength of tone would render this more likely. 'He's a wanted man and we must circulate his description.'

'We have done, sir,' Playford said but the Chief ignored him and went on:

'And when we do find him, my view is we've got enough to charge him with Notley's murder. We know he had ample motive and now the cracking of his alibi means he had opportunity as well. Furthermore, that's supported by the very significant morsel of unburnt blotting-paper you found under the paper-weight. "J.P. 9.45". J.P. clearly stands for Julian Prentice and 9.45 can only refer to the time of an appointment, i.e. Prentice was due to visit Notley at 9.45 that evening.'

On noticing Manton's slightly dubious expression, the Chief quickly added, 'Of course it's not one hundred per cent, but what evidence ever is? Do you agree, Manton?'

'At the moment I think we have a case against him but not a strong one. My feeling is that everything depends on what he says next; and he's bound to say something now that his alibi threatens to go out of the window. As to the present, we've issued his description and it's already appeared in the papers and we've searched all his known haunts during the night without success. The trouble is, I imagine, that someone such as he has a good many hideouts in this town.'

'Something must come through the grapevine,' the Chief said. 'He can't just melt away.'

'He's done it before.'

'Well, he can't do it again. Now off you all go and find him – and let me know the second you've got him under lock and key.'

As the three officers trooped out, Talper turned to Manton and remarked sourly:

'He makes it sound just like hunt the slipper, doesn't he?'

At about the same time that the police conference was beginning, Jason received a telephone call in his office. When informed that the caller had already rung three times in the preceding quarter of an hour, Jason, who was always irritated by phone calls which came before he'd had time to take off his hat and coat, expressed himself forcibly. Then:

'All right,' he said tersely, 'put him through.'

In the split second before Dominic's voice came down the line, he decided to give extremely short shrift to that amiable young puppy, as he had come to regard him. Events were moving fast and he had a headful of problems without adding Dominic's adolescent troubles to them.

'Yes, what do you want? I'm very busy', he said, as soon as the connection was made.

'Can I come and see you at once, Mr. Jason?'

'No, I'm afraid that's out of the question.'

'Please, Mr. Jason. It's something terribly important and I promise not to be long.'

'What's it about?' Jason asked suspiciously, for there was a genuine note of despair in Dominic's tone.

'I can't tell you over the phone, but I terribly need your advice.'

'Where are you speaking from?'

'The public call-box down the street from your office.'

With eyes half-closed behind the usual drift of cigarette smoke, Jason cupped his chin in the telephone mouthpiece and stared unseeingly into the far corner of the room. A second later, he re-focused his gaze and said:

'All right.'

Less than three minutes later Dominic arrived looking rather like a Graham Greene character innocently caught in the moils of international intrigue and relentlessly hunted by police and villains alike. He found Jason sunk in deep concentration, but as he breathlessly closed the door, the solicitor said briskly:

'Well?'

'It's about the Notley murder', Dominic began and then immediately blurted out, 'Well actually I'm not sure how much it's to do with it, though it must be connected somehow. It's awful, I can hardly sleep at nights for worrying about it. . . .' He gave a sigh of anguish. 'Oh, God, I'm afraid I'm not making it very clear, am I?'

'Clear? You haven't spoken two consecutively intelligible words since you entered the room. Pull yourself together.'

Dominic managed to look contrite and took a deep breath.

'I'm sorry, but it's been preying on my mind and getting worse all the time.' He swallowed and in a tremulous voice continued, 'You know about the car that blew up Prentice?' Jason answered by the merest inclination of his head. 'I was the person who hired it from Notley. I was told to and to drive it to Parsonage Road and leave it there.'

'Who told you?' Jason asked quietly, now alert as an electric wire.

'That's the point. I don't know', Dominic said miserably. 'I'd better explain from the beginning. About four days before Prentice came out of prison, I received a typed anonymous letter. It was postmarked Wenley and it referred to my appearance in court and said the writer was sure I would be happy to do him a very small service in order to prevent my father getting to hear of it.' He stopped, attempted a rueful smile and continued, 'It was blackmail. I realized that, but what could I do in the circumstances? The letter went on to say I should go to the public lavatories by the new recreation ground in Wenley at 8.30 p.m. two days later, enter one of the two closets and wait there for my instructions, which, it said, would be short and simple and involve me in nothing criminal, so that I had nothing to worry about.

'The next evening, there was a telephone call and when I picked up the receiver, a voice just said, "Don't forget; eight-thirty tomorrow" and rang off.'

'A male voice?' Jason asked keenly.

'Yes.'

'Disguised.'

'I don't know. It's difficult to say ...'

'But you didn't recognize it?'

'N-no, I didn't really have a chance – and yet there was something about it. But he only spoke half a dozen words and he'd rung off before I properly realized what was happening.' Dominic appeared to cudgel his brains in an effort to be more helpful but eventually went on, 'The next day I went to this rendezvous and a moment or two after I'd entered one of the closets, I heard someone enter the next one. Then a piece of paper was shoved under the partition: it contained instructions about hiring the car from Notley. It was typewritten too and finished by saying that once I'd parked the car in Parsonage Road, I could go home and forget the whole incident.'

'Which you did', Jason remarked tonelessly.

'At the time there didn't seem to be any real harm in it. As the note said, I wasn't required to do anything criminal and quite honestly I was prepared to do it to prevent my father getting to hear about that beastly case. The old boy would have skinned me alive and that would only have been a preliminary measure.' He paused in his digression and went on. 'I should have mentioned that the final part of the instruction was to pass the piece of paper back beneath the partition, having written either "yes" or "no" on it. Then I was to count ten before leaving.'

'Did you catch sight of this person at any time?' Jason asked intently.

'No. As I've said he arrived after I did and while I was counting I heard him leave.'

'He? Him?'

'It was a Gentlemen's Lavatory.'

'But you never actually saw nor heard anything to give you a clue to the person's sex.'

'There was his voice on the phone.'

'No, no,' Jason said impatiently. 'I refer to the person in the lavatory. He or she never spoke while this note-passing took place?'

Dominic looked bewildered and shook his head.

'You mean they were different people?' he asked. But Jason just stared at him with catlike dispassion and said nothing. Finally Dominic said, 'I feel better for having told someone about it at last. What do you think will happen to me?'

'That depends on what you do.'

101

'What do you advise me to do?'

'Go and tell the police', Jason replied without hesitation, while Dominic felt his stomach reel.

Half an hour later he was eagerly scanning Manton's face. Having re-told his story, he awaited official reaction with unmitigated dread and there was nothing in Manton's expression to reassure him.

'And now what about telling me the *whole* truth?' Manton asked, eyeing him with dispassion.

'But I have', Dominic replied in anguish. 'I haven't told you a single thing which isn't the truth.'

'No, I'm not suggesting you have, Mr. Trevane.'

'Then why do you accuse me of lying?'

'I don't. But I do suggest you're still holding something back.'

'I don't understand . . .'

Manton studied him in silence awhile before replying.

'No?' he said at length. 'Let me help you then. You have told me everything *except why* you acted as you did.'

Dominic swallowed with apparent difficulty. He felt as though the walls of the room were closing in on him and when he spoke his voice seemed to him to come from a hundred miles away.

'I was being sort of blackmailed', he said, despairingly.

'Exactly; but what were you being blackmailed about?'

'Do you have to know that?' Manton gave a mandatory nod. 'It won't go any further, will it?'

'You're in no position to strike bargains, Mr. Trevane, so get on and tell me the truth.'

Still Dominic hesitated. Finally, looking a picture of abject despair, he drew a deep breath and said:

'I was an absolute B.F. and once wrote for one of those books – you know, the really filthy sort – and then when the man was prosecuted, I was called to give evidence against him. The police found my name on his mailing list, you see.'

'And you didn't want anyone, particularly your family, to get to know?'

'Yes, so I went to see Mr. Jason before the case and he managed to fix things so that my name didn't come out in open court.'

'Was it Prentice who sold you this book?'

'No, it was in August while he was still in prison. It was a man who has now left the district.'

'But someone apparently saw in it a good opportunity to exert a little pressure on you', Manton observed thoughtfully. A moment later, carefully watching Dominic, he said, 'Was it all this – I mean everything you've now told me – that the police were on no account to find out?'

For a moment Dominic looked puzzled; then with the first glimmer of recollection a gruesome change came over his face. His forehead glistened with great drops of cold sweat and his skin assumed a waxy pallor. Manton could almost smell his fear.

'I think I'm going to be sick', he gasped. He made an effort to get to his feet but swayed dangerously and with an animal grunt toppled from his chair to the floor in a dead faint.

CHAPTER FIFTEEN

MR. QUENCH, the clerk to the Justices, detested fog more than any other natural element. It never failed to disturb his sensitive stomach (or so he imagined), and it was only his very strong sense of duty (or so he again imagined) that caused him to carry on under such adverse conditions.

On arrival in the warm sanctuary of his office, he now removed his smog-mask, hat, coat, scarf and galoshes in that order. He next retired to the small cupboard wash-basin in a corner of the room and there gargled noisily for several minutes. Then he sprayed his mouth with some highly-scented mouthwash which a niece in Syria had sent him the previous Christmas and after that he carefully dabbed at his lips with a soft towel.

His morale thus reinforced he set off down the corridor to take a tally of his Justices. To his surprise and distinct annoyance he found their room empty. It was after a quarter past ten and if work was to start punctually at half past, they should have arrived by now. The roster of the day told him that four were due and it was his intention to constitute two Courts and allocate a couple to adjudicate in each. There was a particularly long and tedious committal for trial case to which he was proposing to assign the two junior J.P.s and his assistant clerk.

He had adumbrated this course to Potts the previous day and obtained his formal approval. But why wasn't Major Potts here now, Mr. Quench pondered irritably. He normally always arrived in good time to be briefed on the morning's list of cases. Not, of course, as to what decision should be reached in any particular case, for that would be most improper, but simply on the foreseeable snags and difficulties that might arise by virtue of dotty defendants or awkward advocates. For example, there was a message from Jason asking that a case in which he was appearing for the defence should be formally remanded to another day as he was unable to attend court this morning.

Mr. Quench had every intention of trying to prod Potts into

refusing this request and, if this failed, of making a fine old song and dance about it in open court when the case was eventually called on. It was a gambit at which he was not unpractised and his remarks on such occasions about discourteous applications, unreasonable lawyers and disruption of Court business were couched in language of shameless hypocrisy and always addressed straight at the Press.

As he peered round the empty room, mentally tut-tutting, his senior assistant hailed him from down the corridor with the news that Potts was on the phone and wished to speak to him urgently. He hurried back to his room.

'Hello, yes, is that Major Potts? I've just been along to your room to see if I could find you. Nothing happened, I hope?'

'I'm afraid I shan't be able to attend court this morning, Mr. Quench.'

'Not be able to', the clerk echoed in a scandalized tone. 'You're not ill, I hope — Oh! but I expect the fog is particularly bad out your way.' He added this rather as a hopeful after-thought since it would have afforded him both solace and a topic for self-congratulation if he could feel that another's sense of duty was not as stern as his own where fog was concerned.

'No, it's neither', Potts replied impatiently. 'Urgent business has arisen which'll prevent my coming.'

'But we agreed yesterday, Major, that we should split the Court into two and that . . .'

'I know, I know. I'm sorry but I can't help it.'

Mr. Quench made cross clucking sounds and then said frostily:

'Very well, I suppose I must rearrange the Court business as best I can, but I really don't know how we shall manage. It's going to be most awkward.' He paused and then in an even frostier tone went on, 'I trust your urgent business will not prevent your attending tomorrow. Remember it's Matrimonial Court day and . . .'

'I'll phone you later about that', Potts broke in and quickly rang off. He turned to leave the room and as he did so, there came to his ears the unmistakable noise of breaking glass. It sounded exactly as if a brick had been hurled through one of the windows and a moment later Eileen came into the study where he had been telephoning. She looked pale and frightened.

'Someone's just thrown this through the dining-room window.'

She held out her right hand and Potts took from it a hard, smooth stone, the size of a duck's egg. Round it was an elastic band.

'This all?' he asked, turning it over and pulling at the band.

'What do you mean?'

'There was obviously something held by the band – probably a piece of paper.'

'That's all I found.'

'We'd better go and have a further look.' As they walked across the hall, he said, 'Were you in the dining-room at the time?'

'No, I was in the kitchen. Mrs. Merlin hasn't come yet and I was washing up the breakfast things. I expect she's been held up by the fog.'

Potts went straight over to the broken window and examined it. The lower pane was smashed and it was apparent that the stone had been thrown at short range. Outside was a three-foot wide flower-bed and this was flanked by a paved path which led from the drive and went round the side of the house to a terrace at the back. Splinters of glass lay on the carpet immediately beneath the window.

'Whereabouts did you find the stone?'

'There', Eileen said, pointing at one of the further legs of the table.

Potts knelt down and, lifting up the white cloth which almost reached to the floor, peered underneath. With a grunt, he plunged an arm out of sight and a moment later stood up holding a scrap of paper in his hand. It was crumpled and several times folded. As he opened it out, Eileen anxiously scanned his face. It seemed ages before it was finally unfolded and he laid it on the table, flattening the corners as he did so.

It was a ruled sheet which had obviously been torn from a notebook and its message which was printed in pencil, read:

'TWISTERS HAD BETTER WATCH OUT FOR
THEMSELVES.'

'What's it mean?' Eileen asked, trying to make her voice sound natural.

'It's a threat, of course. I'll ring up the police.'

'But who's threatening us?'

Potts looked at her thoughtfully and then back at the piece of paper, but he made no answer. They stood in silence, each occupied with their own thoughts for at least a minute and then Eileen said:

'Won't you be late for court?'

'I'm not going today. Thanks to you I've got more urgent things with which to contend.'

He waited for her to give him his cue to explain, but she merely looked at him with calm eyes that blinked mildly behind her spectacles. It was an expression which he had come to find increasingly infuriating and it now had the effect of goading him into a torrent of recrimination.

'Yes, thanks to you.' He hurled the words at her. 'By heaven, what a fuse you so casually lit the first time you ogled Notley: murder, attempted murder and filthy suspicion plastered over us

105

all are just a few of the finer fruits of your beastly, promiscuous, kitchen-scivvy behaviour. And now having as good as wrecked several lives, you just stand there. Can't you say something: speak, blast you.' He took a menacing step toward her, his hands coming up as though going to shake words out of her. But he was met by a look of such icy scorn that he halted in his tracks and gulped. Too late he realized that his vituperation had taken him too far and this time had put him out on a limb from which there was no return – for the simple reason that Eileen was about to sever it.

When she spoke, her voice seemed to come from outer space and Potts felt himself mesmerized by her words.

'Very well, my frightened little husband, now you can have something else to contend with.'

She turned on her heel and moved to the door. As she reached it, he found his voice.

'Wait', he called out. 'Wait or I'll . . .'

Eileen paused and turned her head.

'You'll what?' she asked contemptuously.

'I'll tell the police about you and Notley – *everything*. Don't forget you were an accessory before the fact.'

Ten minutes later he was still standing in the dining-room when he heard her come down the stairs. The front door was opened and shut quietly again. Even in a moment of high drama such as this, Eileen Potts wasn't the type to make noisy demonstrations. Only then did he turn and look out of the window. Fog was eddying through the broken pane and he shivered, feeling suddenly cold.

In less time than it takes to record, Eileen, small suit-case in hand, had disappeared from view.

For several further minutes, Potts continued to stand, slowly becoming conscious of the deep silence all around him. A house had with bewildering suddenness ceased to be a home.

When the telephone rang, he started violently, its insistent call bringing him back to reality. He walked across the hall to answer it. It was only twenty minutes since he had been speaking to Mr. Quench, but it seemed more like twenty years.

'Major Potts wants police protection, sir', Manton said, speaking over the phone to the Chief Constable. 'He says Prentice has threatened him; thrown a stone through one of his windows with a menacing message tied to it.'

'Why wasn't Prentice apprehended when he did it?' the Chief asked, deliberately ignoring the point.

'It's hopeless in this fog, I'm afraid. All he's got to do is keep out of doors and he might just as well be disguised.'

'Apart from this, have you had any other news of him?'

'I'd better explain. There's no positive evidence that *this* was Prentice. No one saw him but he seems to be the most likely person.' Manton went on to relate the whole incident and on his conclusion the Chief remarked:

'Of course it was him. But what does he mean calling Major Potts a twister?'

'One suggestion is that he's referring to the Major's part in getting him sent to prison last time.'

'Is that what the Major himself thinks?'

'Yes.'

'I see. Well, we can't take any risks. I'll arrange for an officer to patrol outside the house; though it'll be more token protection than anything else. If any harm should befall him, you'll probably be finding me back in the Met. as a sergeant. Meanwhile fog or no fog for heaven's sake find Prentice before he commits another murder.'

The day wore slowly on, but there was no further news of him till late afternoon. It was about half past three when a retired police officer, out shopping with his wife, recognized him as he emerged from a public telephone kiosk. Unfortunately it was several moments before the ex-policeman was able to label the face that had seemed familiar to him and by then Prentice had become completely swallowed up again.

Manton swore softly when told this. Then after studying some papers on his desk, he turned to Talper and said:

'Maybe it's only a coincidence but it was the same box that someone used to phone Potts from on the night of Notley's murder.'

CHAPTER SIXTEEN

NIGHT came and gave way to a new day without Prentice being found – without even any further news of him. The only solace that the fresh day brought with it was an amelioration of the weather. Though it was still foggy-inclined, a slight breeze in the night had worked to good effect and visibility was once more reasonable. The forecast, however, was that it would thicken again as the day progressed.

Short of going out on the streets himself and joining the hunt for Prentice, Manton decided that he would be best employed in some intensive indoor cerebration. Things were horribly gummed up, there was no doubt about that and he was beginning to foresee the case being chalked up as one of his failures. It consoled him little that he could apparently be doing no more than he was. Even the scared and pliable Dominic had obstinately refused to say anything further after being resuscitated on the floor of Playford's office. He had come forward to tell the truth – or as much of it as he felt was desirable – but had swooned when Manton had suddenly probed what he was not prepared to divulge and about which he had clearly not expected the police to know.

Despite these set-backs, however, Manton's thoughts were now confidently working on the following premise. That Notley and Prentice were (speaking colloquially and probably literally too) partners in crime: that they had fallen out and therewith each had become a threat to the other – Prentice more so to Notley than the converse. Notley had consequently lost no time in trying to remove Prentice as soon as he came out of prison. On the matter of the attempt to blow up the car, Manton thought it very possible that the hiring gimmick involved Dominic was no more than a double bluff. If Notley proposed to use one of his own cars, he obviously had to conceal the manoeuvre in some way and this he had successfully, if elaborately, achieved. The only alternative would have been to steal a car. STEAL – steal. The word hammered violently at Manton's brain. Could it be that Prentice had been hired by Notley to steal Claudia's car so that Notley could fix it and use it as a murder weapon? But if so, against whom? Not Prentice. The plan had misfired, of course, and Prentice had gone to prison as a result. Thereafter he must have tried to turn the screw on Notley. Manton bit at his lip and returned to his main line of thought.

Notley had failed in his attempt to kill Prentice and Prentice had then murdered Notley to protect his own skin, for he must have realized that the initial failure to kill him could only presage a more determined effort.

So Prentice had killed Notley, having first armed himself with an alibi. But the alibi had also misfired and now Prentice had disappeared for the second time. He had threatened Potts, but why not Jason, the man who had refuted the alibi? As if in answer to this thought, the phone rang and Manton was told that Jason wished to speak to him.

A moment later his soft, insinuating tones came down the line.

'Good morning, Mr. Superintendent. Would I be right in thinking you haven't yet found Julian Prentice?' Quicly he added, 'No, don't answer, because I don't want you to think I'm on a fishing expedition. I'm not. On the contrary, I thought I'd let you have *my* latest information about him – that is unless you really *have* got him in one of your hospitable cells.'

'What is your information?' Manton asked.

'He has failed to keep an appointment with me this morning.'

Manton digested this piece of news in silence; seeking, as was invariable with anything Jason said, for hidden meanings and subtle implications.

'Is there anything very remarkable about that in the circumstances? he asked tentatively. 'He'd more than likely to be seen and caught if he ventured into any of the main streets in broad daylight; and there's usually a policeman on duty in the neighbourhood of your office.'

'I know what you mean, Mr. Superintendent, despite a rather unfortunate ambiguity of expression. I'm afraid, however, you've jumped to a wrong conclusion. You see, I never mentioned my office. No! we were due to meet somewhere far removed from prying eyes and big boots. I won't tell you where but I do assure you it was a genuine arrangement.'

'When was it made?'

'Yesterday.'

'You saw him yesterday?'

I haven't seen him since he left my house somewhat suddenly and angrily the day before', Jason replied with typical obliqueness.

'Did you speak to him on the phone yesterday?'

'I did. Twice in fact.'

'What did he want?'

'He expressed his distress that our respective accounts of the events on the evening of Notley's murder didn't quite tally. I assured him he was unnecessarily perturbed and I offered to meet him and put his mind at rest.'

'And also cook up another story together?' Manton said savagely, for Jason was being odiously smooth.

'Tut, tut, Mr. Scotland Yard Policeman, that's no way to talk to me – particularly on the telephone. Anyone might hear and then think where my reputation would be.'

Manton made a wry face, silently acknowledging the veiled warning. In a carefully casual tone, he said:

'Has he threatened you?'

The idea of this seemed to cause Jason considerable amusement.

'Clients' cross words are one of the occupational hazards of my job', he replied, suddenly turning off his laughter like a light switch. 'Sometimes it takes the form of threats, sometimes of fishwife abuse; but it never does to take it seriously. One has to make allowances.'

'This is rather different. I don't imagine that all your clients have quite so much to feel sore about. From Prentice's angle, you've ratted on him badly.'

'Well, you needn't think *I* want any of your protection', Jason said curtly. 'I'm quite able to deal with Prentice or anyone else who might be so foolish as to try and execute any schoolboy threats.'

With that he rang off. Manton was about to go in search of Sergeant Talper when the phone rang again.

'Major Irwin Potts is here and wants to see you', announced a voice from the inquiry desk downstairs. 'Shall I have him sent up, sir?' Manton hesitated and the voice added in a confidential whisper, 'He seems to be in a bit of a stew, sir. Looks pretty worried if you ask me.'

'O.K.', Manton replied, trusting that it really was the services of a police officer that he needed and not those of a psychiatrist or other professional species of willing listener. While he waited for Potts to be brought up, he fastidiously straighten ed the articles on his desk.

As footsteps approached the door, he got up, straightened his tie and turned to greet his visitor. Although forewarned that Potts seemed worried, Manton was not prepared for the hollow-eyed wreck who now entered. He didn't look as though he had slept for nights and in addition he gave the appearance of being thoroughly scared.

Manton invited him to sit down.

'No further bother, I hope, Major Irwin Potts?' he said, watching him shrewdly.

'Not from Prentice, no.'

'Good. I suspect that throwing a stone through your window was just an hysterical demonstration. He's that type – big gestures but nothing behind them. I expect the officer on duty outside your house has kept him away; that is if he ever thought of returning''

'You're probably right', Potts said abstractedly. There was a silence and then he spoke in such a quiet tone that Manton had to strain to catch his words.

'My wife has left me. She walked out of the house yesterday morning and has vanished.'

Manton's spirit groaned within him. So all Potts wanted after all was to unburden himself of his domestic troubles.

'You don't suspect foul play?' he asked conventionally.

'No, no, I don't believe anything like that has happened to her.' The oddity of his tone made Manton look at him sharply. But he now seemed slumped in a mood of silent despair and sat tugging nervously but viciously at his eyebrows, scattering on the floor around his feet the hairs that succumbed to his assault.

'Forgive me, officer. I'm afraid I'm not at my best today. I still don't know whether I'm doing right in coming to see you, though heaven knows I thought about it for long enough before resolving to do so.'

Manton decided to prompt him, at the same time hoping that he might be spared a saga of marital discord.

'Have you any idea of why she went?'

'We had a row. I blamed her for all our recent troubles.'

'I see', Manton broke in hastily. 'And you've no idea where she's gone?'

'None.'

'Do you think she may have left the district?'

'I don't know. All I do know is that ... that ... that she tried to murder me.'

CHAPTER SEVENTEEN

THERE was a long silence while Manton stared at Potts in patent disbelief. The man was obviously dramatizing and the interview was becoming a nuisance.

'When did she do this? Yesterday? The day before?' he asked, making his tone sound ineffably long-suffering.

Potts looked up in surprise and met Manton's unsympathetic gaze.

'Oh no. It was last March, the time Prentice stole Miss Jason's car. You see, he took it for the express purpose of running me down and killing me.'

'And where does you wife come into this?' Manton asked suspiciously. 'I thought you said it was she who tried to murder you?'

'She was an accessory before the fact. She was in the plot and knew it was going to happen.'

'Why did you never tell the police about this at the time?'

'For the simple reason that I didn't know. I only learnt several months afterwards when she told me.'

'It's curious she should have made such a damaging admission', Manton remarked and went on in a tone of obvious irritation. 'You do realize what you're saying, don't you? That your wife was party to a plot to murder you and then told you about it afterwards?'

'That's the truth.'

'Why didn't you inform the police immediately?'

'Because by then my wife was through with Notley and we had become reconciled.'

'Notley? What's he got to do with it? But even as he spoke, Manton knew the answer.

'It was he who hired Prentice to do the job', Potts said quietly.

'Are you really saying that your wife and Notley put their heads together to murder you and engaged a third person to do it?'

'That's what my wife told me. Except that I gather it was *his* plan and she was the silently concurring partner.'

'But why?'

'They were infatuated with each other and I wouldn't divorce her.'

'It's quite fantastic', Manton said decisively.

'You don't believe me?' Potts asked wearily. 'You didn't know Notley. He was one of the most ruthless men I've ever met.'

This certainly accorded with Manton's own information but he brushed the question aside.

'Do you realize this, Major Potts? That if what you have told me is true, you've pinned on yourself the best motive anyone had for murdering Notley?'

'What's that?'

'Revenge.'

Potts made such a scornful sound that Manton was taken aback.

'If you think I acted out of revenge,' he said, 'I'm surprised at you, because you must obviously be less intelligent than I thought. Is murder ever committed out of revenge these days, except in Soho gang circles? And anyway, why should I wait six months to take it against Notley? If you can make sense of it, go ahead and arrest me and then tell me how I did it.'

But again Manton refused to be drawn.

'Why have you told me all this now?' he asked.

'Because with the disappearance of my wife, I felt the time had come to hold nothing back. My life in Wenley lies about me in ruins and with its disintegration has come the urge to make a clean breast of the past. All my efforts to keep things going normally have failed.' As he finished, he leant back in his chair, obviously exhausted by the strain of his ordeal.

Manton pondered further.

'What motive does Prentice have for wishing you out of the way?' he asked.

'Notley and I were the two persons most concerned in landing him in prison.'

'But that would make it revenge and only a moment ago you discounted revenge as a valid motive for murder outside of Soho.'

Potts gave him a wan smile.

'I agree and the truth is that I don't really believe Prentice's threats against me are serious.'

'But if we put revenge and self-protection aside, what possible motive did anyone have for murdering Notley? What motive did Prentice have, for example?'

'You had better ask Jason that.'

'Meaning?'

'Meaning that a certain type of literary work can be extremely lucrative, and that when crooks fall out . . .'

He eyed Manton meaningly as he let the sentence drift away.

112

CHAPTER EIGHTEEN

ALTHOUGH Potts's visit gave Manton food for thought, it was of no assistance in finding Prentice, who seemed to become more vital to the successful solution of the case with every passing hour. It was like a jigsaw puzzle where the surround of sky and trees, Mary Queen of Scot's bed-chamber, or whatever it may be, gets filled in, but the centre-piece round which the whole puzzle is constructed has been tiresomely lost.

On the morning following the visit, Manton arrived at police headquarters to be handed a letter which was addressed to him personally and bore the Wenley postmark. This much he casually noticed as he slit it open. Inside on a cheap piece of blue-lined notepaper, the following message was printed in clumsily-pencilled capitals:

> IF YOU REALLY WANTS TO FIND PRENTIS,
> TRY LOOKIN DOWN THE WELL. HA! HA!
> YOU KNOWS THE ONE – NEAR GUS' PLACE.

Manton read it through twice and then studied the envelope with new interest. His name and address were scrawled in pencil in an illiterate hand, which, he decided, could easily be a disguised one. It was possible, of course, that the whole thing was a practical joke of the type that feeble or twisted minds delight in playing on the police during their more publicized inquiries. However, it shouldn't be difficult to prove it one way or the other.

He ran up the stairs and along to Playford's office where he found the inspector carefully crumbling a piece of bread on the window-sill watched by a beady-eyed robin.

'Sorry to frighten away your friend,' Manton said as the bird took to flight, 'but this may be important.' He handed the note to Playford and, giving him a moment to read it, said, 'Where's this well?'

Playford scratched at his forehead.

'It must refer to the one in Wybrow Park. If you go on down that road past Jason's house you come to a sort of small park. Actually it's now more like a wilderness; nothing but overgrown shrubs and trees and the grass half-way up your legs. It was originally intended for the residents in that road and each had a key, but the gate has long since disappeared and apart from a few amorous couples in the long summer evenings, no one uses it.

In the middle, there's an old well. I say old, though it's still got water in it and is supposed to be fairly deep. It got to be rather an attraction for kiddies and because it was obviously dangerous, the council stuck a wire fence round it. I think they were afraid that some little horror would topple in one day and they'd then be sued for thousands of pounds.'

'Got your car outside?' Manton asked quickly before Playford could expatiate further on the history of the well. 'Good, let's go at once then. We needn't take anyone else. If we find anything, we can send back.'

About a quarter of an hour later, Playford parked his small car at the entrance to the once private park, in which the road petered out. He and Manton immediately got out and walked between the dang rously dilapidated high brick pillars which had once supported two massive iron gates.

Once inside, the asphalt path, which gave the impression of having been ploughed up and sown with a wide selection of hardy weeds, branched; one fork going off to the left and one to the right. Immediately ahead was a thick screen of tangled bushes.

'I think this way'll be best', Playford said, taking the left fork. 'The well is only just the other side of that jungle.'

Fifteen yards along, he left the path and picked his way through the long grass. It was extremely wet and he lifted his feet with exaggerated care to try and avoid getting soaked. It was a futile endeavour which Manton didn't attempt to emulate.

The fence round the well was about twelve feet out from the rim and consisted of a triple coil of dannert wire. Large sections of it were completely covered by vegetation, but at a spot on the far side of the well from the entrance to the park, it was beaten down and the grass in the vicinity showed that there had been recent foot traffic which had arrived from the right fork.

'We must get in somewhere else', Manton said. 'Can't risk messing up those other tracks until they've been photographed and carefully examined. Got a shovel in your car?'

'Yes', Payford replied as though it was unthinkable that anyone should go anywhere without one. 'I'll fetch it.'

While he was away, Manton walked stealthily round the perimeter, peering in at the well rather like a cautious visitor examining the crater of an untrustworthy volcano. He reckoned the parapet to be approximately eighteen inches high all round except for the part opposite where the tracks lay. Here there was an arc of about three feet where the top row of bricks had disappeared, leaving loose mortar, weeds and an air of unsafety. He noticed that the grass between the wire and the well at this point was heavily crushed and that there appeared to be recent score marks on the outside of the brick parapet. He was trying to gauge the diameter of the well when Playford returned, shovel in hand.

'Let's batter our way in here', Manton said, indicating a point round the other side.

The fence, which was old and unmaintained, could offer no real resistance to the prodigious blows that Inspector Playford rained upon it and in next to no time it was sufficiently flattened to allow them a relatively easy crossing. Relatively, since one strand sprang viciously at Playford and tore a neat triangle out of his raincoat. Cursing fluently, he freed himself.

Once over the obstacle Manton strode four paces to the edge of the well and looked down.

'Here, I've brought a torch', Playford said joining him and directing the beam down into the gloomy depths.

Some thirty feet below they could see the still oily surface of the water, uninviting and eerily sinister. Manton selected a small piece of mortar and holding his arm straight out, dropped it. There was a plop. The water gently rippled but revealed none of its secrets.

'What depth is the water?' he asked.

'About ten feet, I believe', Playford replied.

They moved carefully round the edge and got as close to the damaged portion of the parapet as they could without interfering with the marks left by the other recent visitors. Manton gazed at it hard, moving his head this way and that to get a better view.

'Do you see anything along the top there, just past that loose-looking brick?' he asked suddenly, making room for Playford.

'Looks like red marks', Playford said, straightening up. 'Blood?'

Manton nodded.

'Without any doubt, I think. We'd better get help immediately. We'll need rope and grappling gear to search the well and you'd also better bring a photographer back with you. We'll have to have the whole area photographed. I'm going to snoop about some more while you're away. Oh, and warn Dr. Nation that we shall probably want him along here soon, if we find what we expect.'

With Playford's departure, Manton decided to investigate the other side of the well where the surround was considerably more overgrown. Indeed, it looked to be a mass of uncompromising bramble bushes which grew up to the edge of the well and at points hung over it.

Treading his way carefully and keeping his eyes well skinned, he reached the far side to find that the brambles completely blocked his path, stretching as they did from the edge of the well right back to the wire fence. Fetching a stick, he parted them and peered in at various places. The third time he did so, the bush gaped open as though used to such treatment. About two feet in, he was able to see a mysterious mound. It was covered with earth, sticks and leaves, but there was something infinitely sinister about its shape – which was that of a coffin. He prodded at it and his stick struck against something hard and metallic.

His heartbeats quickened as with terrier instincts aroused he clambered into the bush heedless of rips and scratches. Was this after all where Prentice had been unceremoniously laid to rest? Murdered and then dumped to rot with the leaves and other vegetation? In another few moments he would know – know whether a search of the well itself would still be necessary. Quite suddenly another thought scudded across his mind. What if it wasn't Prentice's body that lay at his feet? Prentice wasn't the only person who had mysteriously vanished. Supposing it were to be Eileen Potts's lifeless face that looked up into his?

Feverishly he swept at the top of the mound with his bare hands to reveal a long tin trunk. For one brief moment he knelt before it in motionless poise while he summoned up all his resolution. Then, gritting his teeth, he wrenched open the lid. Neat piles of innocent-looking school exercise books met his astonished gaze. There were dozens of them. Almost gingerly he picked one up and it was then he knew exactly what he had stumbled on – a well-stocked cache of pornographic books.

·   ·   ·   ·   ·

The task of dragging a well was new to Manton and proved to be difficult, exasperating and grisly in the extreme. It was early afternoon before it was completed and Julian Prentice, unattractive in life but infinitely more so in death, lay on the ground.

CHAPTER NINETEEN

NEWS spreads fast and long before Prentice's body had been recovered, an ever-growing knot of curious by-standers gathered round the entrance to the park. On Manton's orders, they were kept out and thanks to the bushes which effectively screened off the well from the road outside, the police were able to work in complete privacy. There weren't even any rooftops in the vicinity to challenge the ingenuity of adventurous Press photographers with telescopic lenses.

Dr. Nation bent over the body.

'I should say he died of drowning', he announced. 'He shows all the external symptoms, but the sooner you get him to the mortuary, the sooner I'll confirm that.'

'What do you make of those lacerations on the back of his hands?' Manton asked.

Dr. Nation looked at them carefully and then at the bloodstains on the rim of the well, to which Manton had earlier drawn his attention. Speaking slowly he said:

'I should guess that after being pushed in he managed to save himself for a time by clutching hold of the top and that his murderer was forced to belabour his hands to make him let go. I should be surprised if some of the metacarpal bones aren't fractured. These ones, here', he added, indicating behind his knuckles. 'Nasty thought, isn't it?' Manton nodded grimly and the pathologist went on, 'If you search further, you'll probably find the weapon that was used – a good stout stick or something of that sort. Most likely it followed Prentice down the well.'

'If it was a piece of wood, it should have floated', Manton said.

'Could have been a length of metal.' Dr. Nation looked about him. 'What about those iron pegs in the fence? One of them would have been handier still and I notice that there are a number missing.'

Manton peered dubiously over the edge and said:

'I reckon we'll have to send down a diver.' He turned to Sergeant Talper and continued, 'You carry on here and see things cleared up. Inspector Playford and I are off to find Jason.'

It was only a three-minute walk to Jason's house, but as was to be expected at half past three on a week-day afternoon he was not at home. Brushing aside the old housekeeper's querulous protests, Manton used the phone in the hall to speak to him at his office.

He at first strenuously demurred about returning home forthwith but when Manton firmly stated the alternative, he agreed to come and arrived a quarter of an hour later looking flushed and angry.

He stalked into the drawing-room where the two officers were waiting and said:

'This is outrageous, ordering me about in this fashion and threatening to turn my office inside out if I don't choose to come running to you. Let me tell you, Mr. Policeman, that were it not for the fact I don't trust you alone in my house, I'd never have come.' His cold and almost crocodile eyes surveyed them both.

'Play-acting', said Manton quietly. 'That's all you're doing, Mr. Jason. You've returned because you knew it was the only alternative to an unpleasant scene in your office with clients around. It was extremely thoughtful of us to give you the opportunity of facing the music here rather than there, so cease your blustering, bluffing nonsense and tell me where you were the evening before last.'

'Why should I?'

'Because Prentice's dead body has just been fished out of a nearby well and the indications are that he'd been in it for about forty hours.'

This was merely intelligent guesswork on Manton's part, since Dr. Nation had declined to give any estimated time of death until he had completed his full post-mortem examination.

'You're asking me to clear myself, eh?' Jason said softly. Almost as a dreamy afterthought he added, 'Or more likely you're hoping I'll incriminate myself.' He paused and then went on, 'I was out, Mr. Superintendent. My daughter and I motored over to Brailsford to have dinner with an old cousin.'

'How far is that?'

'A good forty miles', he replied with a jeering expression. 'We went straight from the office and I got home shortly after two o'clock in the morning – yesterday morning that is. My daughter stopped with the relative and is returning home this evening.'

'What time did you leave Brailsford to drive back?'

'Just before 1 a.m.'

'Did you come straight back?'

'I did; put the car away and went to bed.'

'Can you give me this cousin's name and address?'

'Miss Louisa Cox, 42 Blossom Avenue, Brailsford. Actually, she's a distant cousin of my wife's side if you want to look her up in the family tree', he said with an amused smile, which did nothing to reassure Manton.

There was something distinctly odd in the change which had come over him in the short time since the interview began and Manton felt puzzled. His alibi had come out almost too pat and for the moment there appeared to be nothing further that could be usefully achieved by prolonging the visit. After a few more questions which elicited nothing new, they departed. As they walked to the door, Manton was conscious of Jason's ironical glance which made him feel certain that the solicitor knew all about the cache of books and was silently mocking him for his impotence to carry the battle of wits any further.

A quick dash in the car brought them to Abbotts Road and Potts's house. They found him mooching about in the garden at the rear: if anything, he seemed more worn and strained than he had the previous day when he called at police headquarters. He was abstractedly pinching off dead blooms and looked startled as Manton and Playford came round the side of the house, having received no answer at the front door.

'My doctor has advised me to spend a few days at home', he said in a tired voice. 'He says I'm thoroughly run down and he's given me a sleeping draught. I don't think I've slept at all since my wife went. Have you any news of her for me?'

118

Manton shook his head and said:

'Major Irwin Potts, would you care to tell us where you were between six o'clock and midnight the evening before last?'

Potts took a deep breath before replying as if this was needed to master his nerves.

'I was at home. But why do you want to know?'

'Prentice has been found murdered.'

'I see; and you think I may have killed him?'

'We have to explore every possibility', Manton said evenly. 'Is there anyone who can corroborate that you were at home the whole evening?'

'Have you asked the constable who was supposed to be guarding me at the time?'

'He only patrols up and down the road. Even if he never saw anyone enter or leave the house, it wouldn't be conclusive.'

'Then I'm afraid you only have my word for it.'

'What were you doing at home?'

'Trying to take my mind off my troubles. I watched television, read a little and generally pottered about feeling miserable and lonely.'

Manton stared vacantly down the garden, lost in apparent contemplation of Pott's piteous plight. The other two men awaited his lead and as Potts stooped to pick up a small trowel that lay at his feet, Manton abruptly focused his gaze on his hands and said:

'How did you get those scratches? Would you mind holding your hands out for a moment?' Potts complied and the officers could see a number of abrasions on both hands, mostly on the backs. Manton looked up. 'Well?'

'I got them cutting a hedge: that one over there', he said, pointing to a recently trimmed line of thick privet. 'It's a particularly tough hedge, and I'm not very expert.'

'May I see the clothes you were wearing at the time?'

Potts seemed in no way put out by this request and indeed gave the impression of someone whose spirit has evaporated, leaving him without will or resistance.

'I'll go and get them', he replied.

'If you don't mind, I'll come with you', Manton said firmly and followed him into the house.

In the bedroom, Potts slid open the doors of a long hanging cupboard and flicked at the sleeve of a sports jacket.

'I was wearing that and also those trousers.'

Manton took the coat-hanger off the rail and examined the two garments over by the window.

'What shirt were you wearing?'

Potts shrugged and looked across at a wicker clothes-basket in

119

the far corner of the room. Manton went over to it. The first thing he extracted was an old khaki shirt.

'This one?' he asked laconically and Potts nodded. He looked at it carefully and said, 'There appear to be bloodstains on the cuffs of the shirt and also of the jacket. It looks also as though the jacket and the trousers have been nicked by something like barbed wire or a bramble.' Potts said nothing but stared at him dully. Manton continued, 'I'm afraid I must take possession of these garments, Major Potts; that is unless you have any objection to my doing so.' But still he said nothing and Manton and Playford left him standing dazed and forlorn in the middle of the bedroom.

    .   .   .   .   .

There ensued a period of intense activity which resulted in the Chief Constable, Manton, Playford and Talper setting off by car for London early the next morning.

They drove first to Scotland Yard, where following a conference with the Assistant Commissioner (Crime), they were joined by him in a visit to the Director of Public Prosecutions Department. Here, a larger and much more protracted conference took place which was attended by the Director himself, the Deputy Director, an Assistant Director and a senior member of the legal staff who would be deputed to handle the case thereafter.

A full discussion left no one in any doubt about its difficulties. While the police had secretly hoped that the legal pundits might be able to reassure them on the matter of evidence and proclaim it stronger than it seemed, the latter for their part – and especially the senior legal assistant who from then on would be bearing the daily brunt of the case – fervently prayed that some additional and conclusive pieces of proof might come to light before the case had to be presented in court.

However practised an advocate may become at making bricks from an inadequate supply of straw, he is naturally happier when he has an abundance of the stuff. It means less effort and better bricks.

As they drove away from the D.P.P.'s office, the Chief Constable alone seemed to be without a care. He was a man who tended – if another metaphor may be pursued – to ignore the individual trees and see only the complete wood; although he had been known on occasions to deceive himself quite grossly about its shape. Simplification of a problem may be a considerable asset, but over-simplification has its inherent dangers.

'You can't always expect to have a one hundred per cent proof-positive case', he said to Manton, who sat beside him in the back of the car sunk in silent melancholy. 'And certainly no one can say that we have no evidence against the man.'

'I know', Manton said with a heavy sigh. 'Yet I can't help feeling that events have now taken control of themselves and we're being left to keep up with them as best we can.'

'Nonsense', retorted the Chief briskly, but in a tone which was not intended to be offensive. 'Forget about the complicating side-issues, for, I tell you, they're just so many red-herrings – juicy outsize ones, some of them, I agree. Concentrate on the main stream of evidence we've got. It looks to me like making a nice well-rounded case.'

For Manton, much of the well-rounded case might not stand up to detailed cross-examination and the so-called main stream of evidence was full of treacherous eddies. These thoughts, however, he prudently kept to himself.

Within an hour of their arrival back in Wenley, Major Stanley Irwin Potts had been arrested and charged with the murders of Notley and Prentice and also with the attempted murder of Prentice on the day of his release from prison.

He was immediately brought before a special sitting of Wenley Magistrates' Court and, after short evidence of his arrest had been given, was remanded in custody for seven days.

CHAPTER TWENTY

TACTICS play as important a part of forensic contests and their preliminary manoeuvres as in military battles. Thus in the days that followed Potts's arrest much time was spent in debating and deciding what evidence to adduce and to what extent efforts should be made to prove motive or to fill in the background of the case. For this purpose Manton returned to London for two days and spend most of them at the D.P.P.'s office conferring with Mr. Otter who would in due course be presenting the case at the Magistrates' Court.

These preliminary decisions were of considerable importance and could have a vital bearing on the outcome of the case and to refer to them as being tactical in no way connotes anything dishonest or underhand.

It had for example been a tactical decision to charge Potts with the attempted murder of Prentice. On the face of it, this would seem to be a piece of redundant nonsense and further proof that the law is an ass, for what point can there be in charging a person with attempting to murder another, when subsequently he has succeeded in accomplishing the complete act – or so allege the prosecution. The answer is tactics.

121

In the present instance it was recognized that the evidence against Potts of the attempted murder was extremely thin – Mr. Otter preferred to call it non-existent – and that if that matter stood alone, the charge could probably not be sustained. It was generally felt, however, that the same hand had committed all three crimes and that the attempt being the precursor of the other two was inextricably woven into the pattern of the whole. (Manton, while agreeing this, nevertheless had his private reservations about all three offences having necessarily been perpetrated by the same person.) It was obvious that the car explosion was bound to be introduced at some stage of the proceedings and the view was held that the prosecution should boldly grasp that nettle itself and hope for the best.

Mr. Otter sighed and said a trifle sadly:

'I suppose it was silly of me to hope that Potts might say something useful when you arrested him. The trouble is that one gets so used to accused persons making long statements which conveniently fill all the gaps in the case one is presenting against them, that going into court without any admission is like appearing in one's underwear: it becomes difficult to deflect attention from the draught one is feeling.'

Mr. Otter was tall and cadaverous with a mournful expression which was often charmingly transformed by a slow, shy smile. He had many years of experience of prosecuting in cases of every size and degree of complexity and there were few snags which he hadn't met and which his own acquired technique hadn't enabled him to overcome.

'There are of course the oral statements he has made to me on several occasions', Manton replied defensively. 'Some of them are helpful in tying him down to a particular line and his allegation that Prentice tried to run him over and kill him is the only explanation we have of that particular incident. Furthermore, it provides Potts with a motive for his subsequent actions.'

'Yes', Mr. Otter said slowly and then repeated the word in an abstracted tone, indicating either that he had heard and remained unconvinced or that his thoughts were elsewhere. It was impossible to know which. 'What arrangements have been made about the composition of the Court?' he asked a moment later.

'That's not been so difficult as we expected. There are several Justices on the roster who don't know Potts other than by sight – I mean they've no social or business links with him in any way – and four of them are being asked to sit. Mr. Quench, the clerk, who of course knows Potts very well, has arranged for a colleague from a neighbouring town to take the case.'

'Fine. Who is defending him?'

'It's a London firm, sir. I've got the name somewhere amongst my papers.' Manton flicked throught the pages of the file in his lap. 'Yes, here it is, Messrs. HIGHFLIGHT, DONLOW and PEEVE in Lincoln's Inn Fields.'

'Good gracious! – what a ridiculous string of names! Anyway I've never heard of them jointly or severally. I suppose they'll be instructing Counsel.'

'I imagine so, sir.'

'Let's hope it isn't some fire-eater who'll chase us all round the ring.'

'Up till his arrest of course, Potts was a client of Mr. Augustus Jason.'

'So I understand; though it's hardly surprising that he's thrown him overboard now. In any event Jason could no longer act for him with any semblance of propriety.'

'Propriety wouldn't deter Jason', Manton said dryly.

'You feel sure he's in this dirty-book business, don't you?'

Manton nodded.

'I certainly look forward to asking him a few questions about it when this case is all over.'

'Yes', Mr. Otter said in a dreamy drawl as his thoughts drifted elsewhere. 'I suppose you've no news of Mrs. Potts?'

'No. If we don't hear something soon, we shall have to treat her disappearance as a case of suspected foul play.'

Mr. Otter groaned politely.

'What a jolly box of tricks we have. Two victims, the accused's wife mysteriously vanished and a haul of the filthiest books I've seen in many a long day. Incidentally, do you think Potts is involved in the pornography racket?'

'There's no suggestion of it, sir.'

'Pity; it might help if we could introduce them.'

'I don't quite see how . . .'

'No, nor do I. All I mean is that I wish we could either tie them in or exclude all reference to them. As it is they present a monumental hare in the case, which the defence are bound to put up, and then the Court will spend hours coursing after it with unflagging energy and we shall be powerless to prevent them. It's so inevitable as to be depressing. If we could only say, "ignore all this about dirty books since they have absolutely nothing to do with the question of whether Potts is the man who murdered Notley and Prentice". But we can't, because we don't *know* to what extent they *do* have any significance.'

'I agree, sir, they're a tiresome complication, rather like a bit from another puzzle that has got into the wrong box.'

'Exactly', Mr. Otter said solemnly and after a contemplative pause went on, 'What about a date for the hearing?'

'The defence have been in touch with the Justices' clerk and want it as soon as possible. They said it was unthinkable that their client, who was, of course, completely innocent, should be kept in indefinite custody while the police prepared themselves at leisure. They were, I gather, most outspoken and pointed out that if we missed the forthcoming Assizes which start in two weeks' time, the trial couldn't take place for another three months, which would be monstrous.'

Mr. Otter managed to look even more martyred.

'How can we possibly be ready by next week?'

'It'll be a rush, sir.'

'And then have briefs prepared and everything copied and ready for Assizes the following week? It's quite unreasonable.' Manton said nothing and Mr. Otter continued with some bitterness. 'When for any reason we want to expedite the hearing of a case, we're accused of unseemly haste and it's suggested we're unfairly trying to stampede the defence. But when it's the other way round, it's a very different story; then we're a bunch of dilatory bureaucrats who are indifferent to the fate of a pathetic accused pining away in prison while we drink our office tea and dangle him in cruel suspense. Tchah!' Manton grinned and Mr. Otter said resignedly, 'Oh, well, see you one day next week, I suppose. In the meantime, I'm not sure I don't hope that someone will push me down a well.'

CHAPTER TWENTY-ONE

AT ten o'clock on Thursday of the following week, the doors of Wenley Borough Magistrates' Court were opened and a flock of excited spectators, who had been waiting with controlled impatience for several hours, jostled their way forward. The first rude shock of the day came when, after no more than a third of them had been admitted, the remainder suddenly found their way barred.

'Come off it, officer. There's still bags of room inside', said a small man, peeved at finding a large blue arm stuck out level with his chest. The owner of the arm gave him a placid stare but said nothing and the small man, after looking around for moral support, piped up again. 'Come on, can't we go in?'

'What d'y think I'm holding my arm like this for, chum – to let the air circulate more freely?'

'Well, what's up? You've only let about fifty in and there's room for lots more than that.'

'Not today there isn't.'

'What they done then? You don't mean-ter-say none of us aren't going to get in? Why, I've been waiting here hours.'

'That's your look-out, but I doubt whether you'll get in. You'll just have to read about it in the papers.'

'This is a bloody lark', the small man said excitedly. 'What the hell's gone wrong?'

'Nothing's gone wrong, chum; it's merely that the gentlemen of the Press want more space than usual and two rows of the public seats have been requisitioned for them.'

'Gentlemen of the Press?' the small man echoed in a bewildered tone.

'Reporters. Haven't you ever heard of them? I reckon we've got representatives of papers from every continent. This is an important case, you know; you're not the only person interested in it. They'll be wanting to read about it tomorrow over their breakfast eggs in Bombay and Buenos Aires, and in Melbourne and Mobile.' The constable, who had been a merchant seaman before joining the police, would have pursued this geographical alliteration with its maritime flavour almost indefinitely had he not at that moment had to take quick action to deal with a queue jumper. When he turned back the small man had mysteriously disappeared.

Inside the court, reporters were scrumming like a market-day crowd, for despite the additional space allotted them, they found themselves severely cramped. Most of the bother was due to the fact that two who represented South American papers and one who proclaimed allegiance to Radio Andorra insisted upon having their interpreters beside them. It could only have been a coincidence that these were three decorative girls with kittenish dispositions.

The court reporter of the *Wenley Evening Post* who had appointed himself the unofficial leader of the party was fussily explaining the procedure to two American newspapermen who were inclined to return straight to London on learning that there would be no robed or bewigged judges and barristers and not a sign of a black cap.

'This is what is called a preliminary hearing before examining Justices', explained the *Wenley Evening Post* man. 'The court simply have to decide whether or not there is sufficient evidence to justify his committal to the Assizes: whether there's what we call a *prima facie* case, which means evidence upon which a jury acting reasonably could convict.' The two Americans yawned in unison.

'How long'll it be before he goes on the witness-stand?' one asked in a bored tone.

'Potts? It will be most unusual if he gives evidence at this court. They always reserve their defence and . . .'

'Then what the heck *is* going to happen?' interrupted the other, bitterly regretting his visit to Wenley. He had never liked courts anyway, since a certain unfortunate experience.

The *Wenley Evening Post* man warmly embraced the opportunity of further explanation.

'All the evidence for the crown will be given and will be written down by the clerk who . . .'

'Who's that guy with the great fuzzy moustache?' asked the first one, rudely butting in. 'Looks a perfectly wizard type', he added in an exaggerated accent which he fondly believed to be an Oxford one.

It was in fact Mr. Lovejohn, the clerk from the neighbouring town whom Mr. Quench had asked to act for him. Mr. Lovejohn, unlike Mr. Quench, was not a full-time clerk to Justices and had a pleasantly typical country solicitor's practice about ten miles from Wenley. He bore no physical resemblance to any accepted legal type and would indeed have found it difficult to explain how he had ever come to drift into the profession. His conversation matched his appearance and could be described as toned-down wartime R.A.F. style.

'My name's Lovejohn; you the D.P.P.'s bloke?' he asked, approaching Mr. Otter who was arranging his papers. The two men shook hands. 'Hope you're not going to shoot any fast ones at me, old boy. Fairly straightforward though, isn't it?'

'No, not very', Mr. Otter replied discouragingly.

'Well, I'll do my best but don't bark at me or get cross, will you, old boy? Actually, Mr. Quench said he'd come along and sit in the wings to see things went tickerty-boo.'

He moved along to have a word with the Counsel who was appearing for Potts. This was Mr. Filby, a capable and respected member of the circuit, whose small military ginger moustache and crisp, no-nonsense-now voice frequently achieved better results with witnesses and juries than the rich, well-modulated and over-done tones, so carefully cultivated by many advocates, which tend to remind one of a strong tide of treacle. Mr. Filby was in deep consultation with Mr. Peeve, his instructing solicitor and, after waiting a few moments without getting any attention, Mr. Lovejohn cleared his throat.

'Sorry to interrupt, old boy, but I'm Lovejohn. I'm sitting as clerk today.'

'How do you do', said Mr. Filby, holding out his hand and surveying Mr. Lovejohn with shrewd, unsmiling eyes. 'This is Mr. Peeve, my instructing solicitor.'

'Are you ready to start?' Mr. Lovejohn asked.

'Yes.'

'No difficulties about the case, are there?' he continued hopefully.

'I shall be cross-examining, if that's what you mean. More than that I can't say at the moment. It all depends what our friend along there produces out of the hat.' He waved a hand in Mr.

Otter's direction and, lowering his voice, added, 'I shall almost certainly be making a submission and I *may* even call evidence at this court.'

'Golly', said Mr. Lovejohn, going distinctly pale at the unwelcome news. That this was going to be no rubber-stamp committal case was abundantly clear. Oh well, it would all sort itself out provided he applied the advice he himself was wont to offer to those whose problems were particularly knotty. 'Let it ride, old boy', he would say brightly – and very often they did with great success.

Mr. Lovejohn retired to the Magistrates' room and a moment later the Court Inspector called out, 'Quiet. Stand, please', as the four Justices came on to the Bench and Mr. Lovejohn took his place below the chairman, who on this occasion was a local brewer. He was accompanied by a retired schoolmaster, a doctor's wife and an ex-postman.

Taking their seats, they blinked uncomfortably under the intense scrutiny of a packed court. The doctor's wife in her mind's eye already saw an unkind description of her slightly ridiculous hat appearing in some faraway foreign newspaper and wished she had played safer and worn a more subdued one.

Suddenly a long piercing whistle filled the court and people stared at each other in startled surprise.

'It's the new loudspeaker system', hissed the Court Inspector to Mr. Lovejohn, who was looking nonplussed and helpless. Happily as he spoke, the whistling stopped.

For years there had been complaints about the acoustics of the court and it was a pure coincidence (after the baptismal whistling one hesitates to say a 'happy' one) that an elaborate and expensive system of microphones and speakers had been installed in time for the case, the work having been completed that very week. Microphones bristled everywhere. There was one in front of the chairman's nose, one for the clerk, one on the ledge of the witness-box, one in the dock and two for the use of advocates. What wasn't readily apparent was where the voices emerged; only that they did so with powerful effect.

Mr. Lovejohn rose to his feet and after intercepting a nervous nod from the chairman, said:

'Put up Stanley Irwin Potts.'

There were distant rumbling sounds beneath the court and then Potts appeared out of the floor of the dock and stepped to the front. He carefully avoided looking at his erstwhile colleagues on the Bench and focused his attention on the high window above their heads. It was a week since his last appearance in public and an astonishing change had come over him in that time. He now looked fit and confident and more boyish than ever. In fact he was a live tribute to the restorative atmosphere of Wenley Prison where he'd been lodged.

'Is your name Stanley Irwin Potts?' asked Mr. Lovejohn and without waiting for an answer, went on, 'You know the charges against you?' Potts nodded. 'Then there's no need for me to read them out to you at this stage.' This brought forth faintly mutinous mutterings from the Press benches and Mr. Lovejohn hastily added, 'Well, perhaps it would be better if I reminded you of them after all.'

He seemed, however, to experience some difficulty in reading out the three charges and managed to make it sound as though he was translating them from an unusual foreign language as he went along. The simple explanation was a combination of nerves and the tiresome writing of the person who had made out the charge sheet. When, at last, he had stumbled through to the end, he said, 'Sit down and listen to the evidence. All witnesses out of court, please. Yes, Mr. Otter', he added, giving the Director of Public Prosecutions' representative his entry cue.

Mr. Otter rose to his feet, lightly brushed a stray wisp of hair off his forehead and waited for complete silence before beginning his opening speech. It lasted exactly thirty-five minutes and was a lucid, carefully prepared exposition of the evidence in respect of each charge. He made no attempt to suppress the weaknesses in his case, but contrived to draw attention to them in such a way that they appeared to be of relative insignificance compared with the strong points which he spot-lighted with subtle pauses and effective changes of inflexion.

While he spoke, the Press scribbled hard (including several whose deficient understanding of English appeared to be no handicap); the four Justices took copious notes in painstaking longhand; and Mr. Filby jotted down an odd word or two from time to time and carefully ringed or underlined the result in red. Beside him a girl shorthand-writer from Mr. Peeve's office was taking a complete note of the opening and on his other side Mr. Peeve himself was also rapidly filling up the pages of an exercise book. Mr. Lovejohn surveyed the scene and uncrossed his fingers: at least, he congratulated himself, it had got off to a rattling good start.

Mr. Otter was nearing the end of his speech.

'. . . If someone deliberately locks another in a room and then introduces into that room an inflammable spirit such as petrol, knowing that it will almost certainly become ignited – and indeed intending that it shall – and it does become ignited and the person is burnt to death in consequence thereof, then clearly that in law is murder, for every man is presumed to intend the natural and probable consequences of his acts. In this case the only possible presumption is that the person who did that fearful thing in-

128

tended to kill Notley. What you will have to decide is whether the evidence satisfies you that it was this accused who did it, though the prosecution submit that there is a clear *prima facie* case against him on that and the other two charges to which I have already referred.

'And with those observations, sir, I will now call the evidence before you.'

The first two witnesses were a detective-sergeant who produced a large album of excellent photographs and a surveyor from the Borough Engineer's Department who produced an unwieldy plan of Wenley with, indicated upon it in red ink, the case's landmarks.

While Mr. Filby was cross-examining one of these witnesses, Mr. Otter turned to the Court Inspector beside him and said:

'Who's that at the end of the row; the chap on the left of Mr. Peeve?'

'That is the egregious Mr. Augustus Jason', the inspector replied with a pleased smirk'.

'What's he doing here?'

'I'll go and ask him', the inspector said and tiptoed round the back of the dock. When he returned he whispered into Mr. Otter's ear, 'Says he's holding a watching brief for an interested party.'

'Who?'

'He didn't say and he certainly wouldn't have told me if I'd asked him.'

Mr. Otter studied Jason covertly. He was sitting back with his hands in his trouser pockets. On the table before him was a file of papers – face down. His expression was inscrutable as he shamelessly and artfully studied Mr. Peeve's papers under cover of his left elbow.

The plan drawer left the witness-box and Mr. Otter rose once more to his feet.

'Dominic Trevane', he said and the officer on door duty at the back of the court repeated the name outside. A moment later Dominic entered.

With the conclusion of Mr. Otter's opening speech, there had been a wild surge out of court by the Press to telephone their first instalments to impatient editors. With Dominic's arrival in the witness-box, however, they started to reappear in the eternal hope of a telling phrase which would provide the morrow's headlines.

Dominic took the oath with a nervous tremor in his voice and turned to face Mr. Otter. He was dressed in a sober blue suit and wore a stiff white collar which was a size too small. The effect of this was to enhance both the glow of his complexion and his general apprehensiveness. His attractively unruly forelock was plastered back and he looked as uncomfortable as a beach-comber in knee-breeches and silver-buckle shoes.

Mr. Otter's questions were asked in a kindly, persuasive tone for which Dominic was grateful, though he knew the worst was yet to come and he shivered as he glanced at Mr. Filby patiently biding his time.

'Thank you, Mr. Trevane', Mr. Otter said at last and sat down. Dominic watched fascinated as Mr. Filby got to his feet and fixing him with a steely look fired his first question.

'Am I right in saying, Mr. Trevane, that you have not the slightest idea who it was that made the lavatory rendezvous with you?'

'No, sir.'

'Or do you mean "yes"?'

'I . . . er . . . I mean I don't know who it was, sir.'

Mr. Filby accepted the correction with a nod.

'And the only time you heard this person's voice was when he – I gather you think it was a male voice – phoned you at your home the previous evening?'

'Yes, sir.'

'I think you said the voice was muffled?'

'Yes, it definitely was.'

'Deliberately so or on account of telephone atmospheric?'

'Well . . . it just sounded sort of . . . muffled.'

'Of course, if it had been Major Irwin Potts speaking in his normal voice, you still would not have known who it was?'

'No, sir.'

'Because at that time you had never heard his voice?'

'That's right, sir.'

'So if it *had* been he, there would have been no point in his disguising his voice since you wouldn't have recognized it anyway. That's right, isn't it?'

'Yes, sir', Dominic said, slightly dazed by the relentless pressure of the questions.

Mr. Filby gave one of the brisk little nods with which he was wont to acknowledge a witness's reply that suited him. His brow deeply furrowed in concentration, he stared at the table in front of him. Then looking up at Dominic again, he said carefully:

'During the lavatory meeting this person never spoke at all?'

'No, sir.'

'It was suggested by my learned friend in opening that the reason for this was to preclude any possibility of your recognizing the voice, should you hear it again. Do you agree with that?'

'Yes, I suppose so.'

'Mmm, I thought you would. But do you also agree, Mr. Trevane, that it's very much more likely he didn't speak in order to prevent your recognizing a voice which you *already knew*?'

Dominic stared with the startled air of a conjurer's stooge having livestock materialized at the end of his nose and Mr. Otter rose to his feet.

'Really I don't think that's a question for the witness', he said deprecatingly. 'It's not for Mr. Trevane to agree or disagree with defence theories.'

Mr. Lovejohn looked apprehensively at Mr. Filby who much to his relief said crisply:

'I've made my point.' And with that sat down.

As Dominic left the box, his ordeal over (or so he hoped), Jason motioned him to take a seat immediately behind where he was sitting.

Claudia was the next witness, being called as the last person to have seen Notley alive. She gave her evidence in a composed manner and carefully avoided looking at either her father or Dominic. Jason, himself, had sat almost motionless since the case started and only his strangely inhuman eyes moved to show how alert were all his senses and never more so than while his daughter was in the witness-box.

'Tell me, Miss Jason,' said Mr. Filby rising to cross-examine her, 'who it was you saw when you were on the pavement outside the hotel just before you and Notley parted company and he was murdered?'

'I don't follow you.'

'Don't you? It's quite a simple question. Do you wish me to repeat it?'

There followed one of those deep still silences which last only a moment but are so charged with tension that one is afterwards left helplessly trying to recreate them in one's mind in order to pinpoint their significance.

Claudia shrugged her shoulders and the moment was gone.

'I didn't see anyone', she replied coolly.

'Are you sure of that?'

'Of course I am.'

'Do you know a Mr. Joseph Camara?'

'No.'

'He's the night porter at the hotel.'

'Oh! Well perhaps I know him by sight, but I had no idea of his name.'

'You see, Miss Jason, I've asked you these questions because he says that he happened to notice your expression when you were on the pavement and it looked exactly as though you'd suddenly seen someone you knew?'

'He's wrong.'

'Someone whose presence seemed to startle and annoy you?'

'Mr. Notley's was beginning to annoy me.'

'No, Miss Jason, this was someone else.'

131

The moment of tension was back and Mr. Filby quickly resumed his seat so that it fell to Mr. Otter to break the spell and call for the next witness. Meanwhile Claudia went and sat next to Dominic who gave her a fleeting and uneasy smile which she answered by scanning his face with grave eyes. Immediately in front of them Jason continued to sit motionless, taking no notice of either of them.

Thus the day wore on. Witnesses came and departed: advocates bobbed up and down: reporters strolled in and out: the four Justices scribbled away without respite: and the public sat endlessly staring as though participating in an endurance contest.

It was late afternoon before Manton reached the witness-box and started to give his long evidence. The assistant clerk who was taking the depositions on a so-called silent typewriter was by now getting tired and the whole pace of the proceedings had slowed down. Furthermore there is often a degree of tedium in a police officer's evidence, coming as it usually does at the end of a case and disclosing very little that isn't already known. However, when at last Mr. Otter sat down and Mr. Filby came to active life again, people stirred with renewed interest and hope.

It might be added that Mr. Filby was one of the few in court who looked as fresh and vigorous at half past four as he had some six hours earlier.

'Am I right in saying, officer,' he began in his crisp tones, 'that Major Irwin Potts has *never* said one *single* word which could *possibly* be interpreted as any sort of admission of any of these charges?'

'You are, sir.'

'We have heard from your evidence how he told you of Prentice's deliberate attempt to kill him by running him down in a car.'

'Yes, sir.'

'Can I take it you accept that as the truth?'

'That's not for me to say, sir.'

'Are you not satisfied it's the truth?'

'It could be, sir.'

'Not "could be". It is, officer, isn't it?'

Manton made no reply and Mr. Filby went on, 'Very well, let us go step by step. In Notley's safe you found the diary, exhibit thirteen, and somewhere at the end of it, there's a rough road sketch, is there not?'

'Yes, sir.'

'In Notley's handwriting?'

'Yes.'

'Of the area of Major Irwin Potts's home?'

'It could be, sir.'

'Could be?' asked Mr. Filby sharply.

'It appears to be.'

'Thank you. There's the number of his house – twelve – which is in fact situated in relation to a road junction exactly as shown in that sketch?'

'That is so, sir.'

'Now as to the two figures which appear underneath the sketch and about which you profess to be ignorant. I suggest to you, officer, that the figure "one hundred and sixty-five" is near enough the number of yards from the road junction to number twelve?'

'Yes, sir, it is approximately that distance.'

'And the other figure "seventy" is the number of yards from the cross-roads, which are off to the right and not shown, to the Scout hut. Will you accept that from me?' Manton nodded. 'From your inquiries do you know that Major Irwin Potts is an extremely methodical man – almost a slave to routine?'

'I have heard that, sir.'

'Even to the extent of always crossing the road at the same place when he walks home each evening?'

'I didn't know that.'

'On reaching the Scout hut, he used always to cross the road diagonally and arrive on the far side about one hundred and sixty-five yards from his house. Did you know that?'

'I didn't.'

'You follow my question. I'm suggesting that having turned into Abbotts Road at the crossroads he used to walk seventy yards along to the Scout hut and then cross over to the other side at a point a hundred and sixty-five yards from number twelve?'

'I understand, sir, but I didn't know.'

'But you don't dispute what I'm saying?'

'I'm in no position to do so.'

'Very well, let us now turn back to the pages for the week in March where a time appears for each day. There's no more than four minutes between any of them, is there?'

'Correct, sir.'

'And they relate to the week which immediately preceded the one in which Prentice took Miss Jason's car?'

Manton slowly nodded.

'I put it to you that those times were clearly recorded by some-one who spent those five days closely observing Major Irwin Potts's movement and that they represent to the minute the precise hour at which he began to cross the road on the last lap of his journey home on each of those days? Five forty-five, five thirty-eight, five forty-one, etc.?'

All eyes turned expectantly on Manton as the significance of the cross-examination now became more apparent.

'I don't think that is a question I can answer, sir.'

'Of course it isn't,' Mr. Otter murmured audibly.

'Will you agree that exhibit thirteen appears to corroborate what Major Irwin Potts told you?' Mr. Filby pressed.

'Putting it your way, I agree.'

'Well, have you any alternative interpretation of those diary entries?'

'No, sir.'

'Thank you', Mr. Filby said, with one of his nods. 'Now, you have told us you found a piece of scorched paper with J.P. nine-forty-five on it. Whose initials are J.P.?'

'They could be Julian Prentice's.'

'Have you found anyone else with those initials remotely connected with this case?'

'No, sir.'

'And the time – nine-forty-five – was about the hour Notley died?'

'Yes.'

'And the doodle on the same scrap of paper could represent a man being run over by a car?'

Manton looked at it carefully.

'Yes, it could,' he said slowly, 'though that hadn't previously occurred to me.'

'I'm suggesting that scrap of paper clearly indicates that Prentice had an appointment with Notley at nine-forty-five that evening. His initials are on it, the time is on it and finally that doodle confirms that it was Prentice who was in Notley's mind when he was jotting it down. Prentice, the man who had been hired to run over my client in a car?'

Manton made no reply and Mr. Filby went on, 'You also found some pornographic books in Notley's safe?'

'Yes.'

'Prentice was a known pedlar of pornography, wasn't he?'

'He had a conviction for it.'

'Oh, no, officer, that won't do. He was known to be actively involved in the obscene book racket, wasn't he?'

'The police had no positive evidence . . .'

Mr. Filby drummed the table with his fingertips and broke in icily.

'Was he or was he not known – suspected if you prefer it – to be a distributor of pornogrpahy?'

'The police had their suspicions.'

'And against Notley, too?'

'No.'

'But he and Prentice were close associates, were they not?'

'It depends what you mean by associates, sir.'

'Don't fence with me, officer. They were pretty "thick", were they not?'

'Yes.'

'And clearly Prentice wasn't in the obscene book business on his own?'

'Probably not.'

'Amongst the books you found at the well, was there one called' – Mr. Filby glanced down at his papers and read out in clipped tones – '*Curvaceous Christine and the Masochistic Monk*?'

'There was.'

'Was it a thoroughly filthy and revolting book?'

'They were all of that order.'

'Complete, unadulterated pornography?'

'Yes.'

'Have you come across that particular book anywhere else?'

'No', said Manton, puzzled.

Mr. Filby pursed his lips thoughtfully.

'Is it known to you that Major Irwin Potts has taken a prominent part in trying to stamp out this particular form of vice in Wenley?'

'Yes, sir.'

'That when he has adjudicated in such cases in this very court, severe penalties have always been imposed; and more than once he has threatened even severer action in the future?'

'I've been told that, sir.'

'Do you not think *that* may have been the reason someone was so desperately anxious to kill him and devised this diabolical plot to encompass his death and make it appear as an everyday road accident?'

Mr. Otter jumped to his feet.

'Surely that's not a question for this witness', he said in a pained voice. 'It's not for Superintendent Manton to comment on possible motives anyone may have had for acting as they did.'

'Maybe not', Mr. Filby agreed and went on, 'but what I'm suggesting to you, officer, is that this case has nothing to do with cuckolded husbands and revenge, as the prosecution suggest, but arises from one man's expressed intention of stamping out vice and from the internecine gang warfare that a misfired plan precipitated?'

Manton maintained a dignified silence in the face of this artfully rolled-up slab of comment which bore no resemblance to a question. He was conscious, however, of the heightened interest and tension which it had everywhere aroused. Augustus Jason alone remained impassive.

Mr. Filby continued his cross-examination and concluded with questions which underlined Potts's alibi for the evening of Notley's death, coupled with a reminder that it appeared that Prentice had had an appointment with him (Notley) at about the time he must have died.

When he sat down, Mr. Otter rose and said a trifle wearily:

135

'That is the case for the prosecution.'

Immediately Mr. Filby was on his feet again.

'I would be greatly obliged, sir,' he said, addressing the chairman, 'if you would now adjourn till tomorrow so that my instructing solicitor and myself may have a full opportunity of discussing the proper course to take in the light of the evidence which has been given. At the moment I prefer not to indicate what it may be.'

'Very well', the chairman said, opening his mouth for the first time that day. 'We'll adjourn till half past ten tomorrow morning.'

As they threaded their way out of court, Manton turned to Mr. Otter and said:

'Sounds as though they've got something up their sleeve, sir.'

'I'm certain of it and I only wish I had an inkling what it was.' Gloomily he added, 'All we can do is to press on to the end even if our case does crumble about our ears.'

'Do you really think we've got the wrong chap in the dock then?' Manton asked in slight alarm.

'If we have, no one can blame us for it. But the truth is, you know, that circumstantial evidence can deceive as subtly and damnably as a lying eye-witness.'

With this disconcerting observation, Mr. Otter dived into a room labelled BARRISTERS ONLY and left Manton to wonder what unwanted surprised the morrow would spring. He had seldom felt so ill at ease and uncertain about a case.

CHAPTER TWENTY-TWO

THE next morning at Manton's suggestion he and Playford walked to court, since, as he remarked, it would probably be their only opportunity that day of stretching their legs and getting some fresh air.

Sergeant Talper left by car at the same time to go ahead and deal with such routine matters as witnesses expenses and the arrangement of the exhibits, the bulkier of which he carted to and fro in a suit-case with an inviting label of a Lugano hotel on its lid.

'We shall soon know the worst', Playford said as he lumbered along at Manton's side. 'It almost looks as if the defence are going to try and pin it all on to a specific individual, which strikes me as being a very dangerous gambit.'

'It's worse than sitting on dynamite unless you're sure of your ground; and I don't believe that anyone as experienced as Filby would attempt it unless he is convinced he can make the counter-accusation stick.'

'He may of course leave the evidence pointing hard in one direction without actually mentioning any names.'

Manton dodged round a small boy on a tricycle and said:

'I seemed to spend most of last night wondering what we'll do if the Justices discharge Potts and we're left with three unsolved crimes on our hands.'

'It'll be the end of everything', Playford agreed and added, 'We can hardly rush in and arrest someone else on what has emerged so far.'

'No, and that's why I don't think Filby will directly accuse a specific person unless he's got positive evidence to back it up. And if there is evidence, we may be able to act at once.

'But what evidence can he have which we know nothing of?'

'That remains to be seen. For the moment he's got us guessing.'

'Blast him!' Playford said energetically.

'Though it's reasonably obvious,' Manton went on, 'who is being dressed up for the part of villain. What's more it promises to be a nice fit.'

'You really think so?'

Manton nodded.

'Who, more than anyone else, was in a better position to arrange for Claudia Jason's car to be stolen? Who by refuting Prentice's alibi spiked his own? Whose alibi for Prentice's death is so remarkable as to bear all the hallmarks of a conjurer's sleight of hand? And who is quite likely to have been running the obscene book racket as a profitable sideline? The same name offers itself in answer each time.'

'Yes, and also to the question: who was it Claudia Jason was surprised and annoyed to see outside the hotel?'

'In fact,' Manton said, 'it only needs two further bits of evidence to emerge for us to have a case against him.' Playford waited for elucidation and Manton went on, 'Firstly, positive evidence of his presence in the vicinity of Notley's Garage on the night of the murder and secondly of his complicity in the pornography racket.'

Playford was silent for a moment. Then he said:

'As to the first, we'll never learn anything from Claudia Jason; that's quite certain.'

Manton gazed about him and shoving his hands hard down into his overcoat pockets said:

'Well, this promises without any doubt to be as dramatic a morning in court as you or I have known. It's a pity we shan't be able to enjoy it with the same detachment as the gawping public.'

Playford sniffed contemptuously.

'Another month and my chief worry is going to be the amount of greenfly on my chrysanthemums and whether the fish in my pet stream will be biting on this or that day. I'll never set foot inside another court, nor shall I follow modern tradition and off-load a book of memoirs on the public.'

'Congratulations on that anyway', Manton said warmly.

The combined overnight efforts of the world's Press had pro-duced a fantastic throng of people in front of the court, only a fraction of whom had managed to get inside. The great mass just stood and watched the arrival of the leading players in the drama.

'There, that one, he's the Scotland Yard man', Manton heard the inevitable wiseacre say to his neighbour, indicating with a nod of his head a tubby man a few paces ahead of Manton, who turned out to be a drainage expert in the Borough Engineer's Department.

Playford looked about him and made a rough count of the extra constables who had had to be summoned to control the crowd. He sighed and said resignedly:

'Nice day for housebreaking. Next thing some disgruntled ratepayer will write an angry letter to one of the local papers saying it's a scandal that Wenley police are never where they are needed and asking why they can't be employed doing something useful like catching burglars instead of harassing harmless crowds and frustrated motorists.'

'Yes; it's always burglars we're exhorted to go out and catch, rather as if all one had to do was chase them with butterfly nets for a bit of afternoon's sport.'

The two officers pushed their way through the last of the throng and entered the court building. Inside, the tension was almost palpable and there was clearly not one person packed into the court who didn't expect dramatic happenings of some sort, though most had only the haziest notions what they might be.

Mr. Filby came in and nodded formal 'Good-mornings' to Mr. Otter, Mr. Lovejohn and the police officers, but Augustus Jason he studiously ignored. Was this an omen, Manton wondered, as he watched him (Mr. Filby) sit down and unfold the papers of his brief, smoothing them with slow caressing movements of both hands. He must have been aware of the greedy looks focused upon him, but he chose to be stony-faced as a Chancellor of the Exchequer on pre-budget day.

After the Justices had taken their seats and Potts was back in the dock, silence fell swiftly and completely. Mr. Filby rose and without any preamble said in his brisk matter-of-fact tones:

'I shall be calling evidence, sir, including my client. I would, however, ask that I might first call a witness who is here against doctor's advice. I take it there's no objection to such a course.'

He gave Mr. Otter and the Bench a challenging look which brooked no protest and then said, 'Call Mrs. Irwin Potts.'

Manton, Playford and Mr. Otter exchanged quick glances and Manton whispered to the other two, 'So that's what they've had up their sleeve all this time.'

'Part of it, anyway', Mr. Otter replied with deep pessimism.

The Press reporters who had, of course, been aware of Eileen's disappearance and had been titillating the public's palate with some highly-coloured speculation about it since her husband's arrest, now almost set their note-books alight with overworked adjectives as she came into court. They barely waited for her to take the oath scrambling for the telephones.

One look at her standing in the witness-box clutching the ledge for support was sufficient to see that she was indeed far from well. She stared hypnotically at a point on the opposite wall and never shifted her gaze during the whole time she was giving her evidence.

'It's almost as if she's learnt it by heart', Playford whispered in Manton's ear, as she answered Mr. Filby's questions in a mechanical monotone.

Manton leant forward, his eyes and ears determined to miss nothing. Any moment there might be dropped some vital clue, possibly not so much in what she was saying as in what she left unsaid.

'Was there at one time an association between yourself and the late Thomas Notley?' asked Mr. Filby, coming to the crucial topic.

'Yes.'

'Did it finish before his death?'

'Yes – long before.'

'When, Mrs. Irwin Potts?'

'About last April.'

'Which of you took the initiative in breaking it?'

'I did.'

'What was Notley's reaction?'

'He didn't like it.'

'Did he tell you something in a fit of anger about this time?'

'Yes.'

'What was it?'

'That he had paid this man Prentice to kill my husband and make it look like an accident.'

'For what reason?'

'So that we could then get married.'

'Was that the first you knew of this plan to murder your husband?'

'Yes.'

'What was your reaction when he told you?'

139

'I was absolutely horrified and I immediately informed my husband.'

'Did you have anything further to do with Notley after that?'

'No', Eileen said, staring harder than ever at the wall.

At this, Jason slowly raised his eyes to her face; his thoughts, however, remained hidden deep behind an expressionless mask of impassivity. Manton had meanwhile observed that Potts appeared to be as concerned not to look in his wife's direction as she was to avoid looking his way. He sat with his head and hands in an attitude of prayer, gazing blankly at the floor of the dock.

'Did your husband at any time ever threaten to seek revenge against Notley – to kill him for example?'

'Certainly not.'

'And six months later at the time Notley was killed, did your husband have any cause to be jealous of you?'

'None whatsoever.'

'Did he harbour any grudge against Notley?'

'No. That's a ridiculous idea.'

'So the position was, Mrs. Irwin Potts, that your association with this man terminated on your initiative about six months before his death and that your husband entertained no revengeful feelings toward him in October of this year?'

'Exactly.'

'So far as you know, did he have any motive at all for wanting to kill Notley?'

'No, none; and what is more, I'm sure he didn't do it.'

'Pop goes the motive', muttered Playford.

Mr. Otter's heart which had been sinking throughout Eileen's evidence now reached his boots with a small, inaudible plop and he felt a trickle of sweat from his armpits. Like all his colleagues on the Director of Public Prosecutions's staff he seldom had occasion to cross-examine witnesses, appearing as he did only in Magistrates' Courts and then usually to pilot cases on their way to Assizes and Quarter Sessions. He was as experienced in examining witnesses and coaxing their evidence out of them as he was unpractised in cross-examination. What should he now do? was the question which rang like an alarm bell in his head. His feeling of inadequacy was aggravated by the knowledge that, in any event, one can only cross-examine if one has the necessary material and he had none. It would be both inept and futile to get up and ask questions of the variety which invites witnesses to repeat their evidence all over again – often with increased effect. Equally it would be less than helpful to embark upon a series of the I-suggest-it's-all-the-opposite type of question.

All this went through his mind as he rose slowly to his feet and in confident and apparently unperturbed tones said:

'I don't propose to cross-examine at this stage.'

He sat down again in the earnest hope that he had conveyed to the court that, though there was much he could cross-examine Eileen about, he had no desire to waste time with a host of unnecessary questions.

Eileen left the box and, looking neither to left nor right, the court. Mr. Peeve hurried out after her.

'I now call my client', Mr. Filby announced and turning toward the dock gave successive nods to Potts and the witness-box.

The Press benches hummed like a generating station as Potts walked past them. After he had taken the oath, Mr. Filby squared his shoulders and began:

'Is your full name Stanley Irwin Potts?'

'It is.'

'Did you murder Thomas Notley?'

'I did not.'

'Did you murder Julian Prentice?'

'No.'

'Did you attempt to murder Prentice by blowing him up in a car?'

'No.'

Mr. Filby frowned.

'Would you stand a bit closer to the microphone, Major Irwin Potts, or we shan't hear properly. This court seems to swallow up voices', he added with a martyred air, and almost unthinkingly, for laments about court acoustics have beome a ritual with Bench and Bar who secretly enjoy the martyrdom they often affect to suffer. Judges, especially, some of whose hearing is no longer of pristine efficiency, are perpetually enjoining witnesses to speak up 'so that the jury may hear'. The jurors concerned are usually either too bewildered or flattered to notice this little example of judicial slyness.

Potts took a pace nearer the microphone and Mr. Filby embarked on a series of detailed questions to amplify the stark economy of his opening ones. In particular he led him slowly and carefully through his alibi evidence of the events on the night of Notley's murder and Potts repeated exactly what he had told the police in Jason's office that morning which to Manton now seemed a decade ago.

'After you had put down the receiver on this unknown caller, I gather there was a minute or so before the telephone bell rang again?' Mr. Filby recapitulated.

'Yes, but I didn't answer it. I just let it go on ringing until the person must have realized I wasn't going to and gave up.'

'And that was all?'

'Yes.'

'And you were home the whole of that evening?'

'I was. I never left the house at all.'

141

Finally Mr. Filby broached the subject of obscene books and after eliciting from Potts the part he had played in trying to exterminate the racket, went on:

'You heard me ask the superintendent about a book called *Curvaceous Christine and the Masochistic Monk*?'

'I did.'

'Have you ever seen a copy of that book?'

'I have.'

'Where?'

There followed a silence in which Potts, looking extremely uncomfortable, swallowed several times and ran his tongue round his lips.

'Where?' Mr. Filby repeated. Potts looked at him beseechingly and he added, 'I know it's embarrassing to you but I want you to tell the court where you've seen a copy of that book before.'

'It wasn't a single copy, it was a whole pile of them.' Mr. Filby nodded encouragingly and Potts went on, 'I saw them on a table in Mr. Augustus Jason's house.'

Claudia let out a sudden gasp and Manton saw Dominic turn an unbecoming green as he grasped her hand. But Manton now riveted his attention on Jason himself who sat with the sinister stillness of a spider aware of lurking danger.

While the moment of tension still held, Mr. Filby sat down and Mr. Otter, who felt he was swimming against Niagara, just shook his head to indicate he didn't propose to cross-examine. There was general relief when the Justices announced they would adjourn for ten minutes.

Mr. Otter, Manton, Playford and Talper went into an immediate huddle.

'It must go its course and we'll just have to wait and see what happens', Mr. Otter said after a good deal of discussion. 'We obviously can't do anything now. Furthermore I doubt whether there's anything we shall be able to do immediately, when the case is chucked out.'

'But we must, sir', Manton said urgently.

'Any hasty action will only land us in a worse pickle', replied Mr. Otter firmly and Manton felt logically bound to concede this.

'Jason had an accomplice all right and I'm sure I know who it was', Talper said as they were resuming their seats.

Manton nodded.

'I've been thinking so for some time: it helps to explain a lot of things. You mean young Trevane?'

The telephonist who had been on duty in Wenley Exchange on the night of Notley's murder and who was the next witness to be called promised to be something of an anti-climax. He was a

cheerful round-faced little man who answered Mr. Filby's
questions with ease and apparent enjoyment.

It was while he was giving his evidence that Manton felt a tap
on his shoulder and turned to find Dominic crouching behind
him. It was at the same moment that he noticed Jason's place was
empty. He looked quickly around the court but the solicitor had
disappeared.

'May I speak to you outside?' Dominic whispered. 'It's important.'

Manton appeared to weigh his decision and then without a
word slid out of his seat and tiptoed out of court with Dominic
behind him.

Mr. Filby meanwhile concluded his examination-in-chief of
the telephonist and more as a formality than otherwise turned to
Mr. Otter, who to everyone's surprise got up and said:

'Yes, there are one or two questions I'd like to ask this witness.'

Outside the court-room, Manton and Dominic stood in a
recess of the corridor.

'How can you be sure?' Manton asked suspiciously.

'I can't be a hundred per cent, but I'm certain it's the same voice
that telephoned me.'

Manton frowned. Then he said:

'I must get back into court. Wait for me when we adjourn for
lunch.'

Dominic nodded nervously but did not follow him back in.

'But I don't understand why you should have remembered this
conversation in particular', Mr. Otter said with an air of melancholy patience. 'You must have had hundreds of conversations
with subscribers which you don't remember, so why this one?'

'Because I do', the telephonist replied stoutly. 'I mean it was
almost as if he wanted me to remember it; that's why it impressed
itself on my memory.'

'Really, that's most interesting', Mr. Otter remarked.

'Don't comment on the evidence, please', Mr. Filby said tartly.

'As I understand it, this caller told you he'd been speaking to
the accused's number and had been cut off?'

'That's what he said.'

'And what then?'

'He said he'd dialled again and got no answer and so he wanted
me to ring the number from the exchange.'

'Which you did, but also got no answer?'

'No, but I could tell it rang all right. Perhaps there was no one
in', he added helpfully.

'The accused has told us he was at home the whole evening.'

'I can't say anything about that, can I?' the telephonist said with a shrug.

'But if what you tell us happened, how many times would the accused's telephone bell have rung after he had cut the caller off for the first time?'

'Twice, of course. Once when this chap dialled again from the call-box and then when I tried to get through from the exchange.'

'It couldn't have been just once?' Mr. Otter said keenly.

''Course it couldn't', the telephonist said crossly. 'I've already explained to you, once when . . .'

'Yes, yes; thank you', Mr. Otter said quickly and sat down bathed in perspiration.

There ensued a tense and brittle silence which was abruptly broken by a sickening thud as Potts slumped forward and struck his head on the ledge of the dock. A moment later he lurched from view and fell with a shattering crash to the floor.

CHAPTER TWENTY-THREE

A WEEK later, and a few days before the opening of Wenley Assizes. Mr. Otter, Manton, Playford and Talper forgathered in the Chambers of Mr. Thomas Gupp, Q.C., who, with Mr. Dalrymple as his junior, had been briefed to appear for the crown in the case of Regina v. Potts.

The consultation was in progress and Messrs. Gupp and Dalrymple busily scribbled indecipherable notes all over the papers of their briefs as Mr. Otter and Manton answered their queries.

'It seems such a silly little point on which to have got caught out', Mr. Gupp said with the air of one ever puzzled by human folly.

'Yes and no, sir', Manton replied. 'It was a silly mistake, but it was also a very understandable one in the circumstances. You see, after he'd murdered Notley, he had to provide himself with an alibi and support it, if possible, by independent evidence. His alibi was that he'd never left the house that evening; but, seeing that he did, he couldn't be sure someone hadn't tried to phone him while he was out. If they had and it later came out, his lie would be immediately spotlighted. So he conceived the clever idea of making an ally of the telephonist. Alas for him as he stood in the call-box deliberately impressing himself on the man at the exchange, he miscalculated the correct sequence of events in the story he was proposing to put forward.'

'Yes, I follow', Mr. Gupp said. 'Since of course his tale to the telephonist of having been cut off in the middle of a conversation and having dialled the number again without success was a pure fabrication.'

'Exactly, sir. Presumably he listened to his own number ringing as the telephonist was trying to get through and imagined himself at home. The matter then became fixed in his mind that way – namely a single unanswered ringing.'

'Mmm, as you say, Superintendent, a silly but understandable error. One, however, which may well cost him his life.' He turned over a page of his brief and went on, 'Now let me see if I have got the whole picture.

'About a year ago Notley makes a pass at Mrs. Potts and she becomes infatuated with him. The accused refuses to give her a divorce and the unscrupulous Notley thereupon plans to kill him in a faked car accident.'

'If I may interrupt a moment', Mr. Otter said. 'I think it's important to understand that Notley was ultimately driven to desperate measures not so much out of love for Eileen Potts – it wasn't a straightforward David and Uriah story – but out of desire for her money. After all we now know he was a man of straw and that the balloon was likely to go up any time if he couldn't lay his hands on some good hard cash. Of course, once the plan to kill Potts had failed, he dropped her like a bad business deal and sought elsewhere.'

'You don't think he was in love with her, then?' asked Mr. Gupp.

'Certainly not as much as she was with him. Indeed, I doubt whether love is at all the right word to describe his feeling toward her. On the other hand, she remained under his spell to the day of his death. What's more, the accused knew it. He realized that Notley had only to lift his little finger and she'd be at his side, divorce or no divorce. But Notley of course didn't want her at his side without her money too.'

'Mrs. Potts's money seems to have been a powerful influence all through this case', Mr. Dalrymple remarked.

'It was fear of losing it that drove Potts to murder', said Manton. 'All his ambitions depended for their success on having a wealthy wife and without her he was in the gutter. He just couldn't afford to lose her, in fact.'

Mr. Gupp cleared his throat and took command again.

'And so he decided that Notley must be got out of the way. But he also realized that if he was suddenly found crudely murdered he, Potts, would immediately become the prime suspect. Accordingly, he hit upon the ingenious idea of murde ing Prentice in such a manner that everything pointed to Notley as the villain. Unfortunately for him, *his* plan also went astray – incidentally the useful modern motor car seems to have let everyone down in this case: it wouldn't run over Potts and it didn't blow up Prentice properly – though, as was intended, Notley came under immediate suspicion for the crime. Knowing what he did, Notley must have had a pretty good idea that it was Potts who was trying to frame him, and when things began to look really ominous he had a showdown with him. That was at his garage and resulted as we all know in his death.'

'Yes', chimed in Mr. Dalrymple, nodding. 'One gathers that Notley threatened to expose Potts unless he would do something to divert the suspicion which he had so skilfully directed on to him. Potts must have been surprised by Notley's intelligent guesswork and quickly realized how great was his peril.'

'So with commendable opportunism he murdered Notley then and there,' said Mr. Gupp with a rush and continued, 'and as to that I think we're agreed that he probably had no such intention when he first arrived at the garage.' He didn't bother to look round for support but hurried on before anyone had time to interrupt him again. 'Everything immediately pointed to Prentice as the murderer. It was neat that: Notley suspected of the attempt on Prentice's life and then Prentice of turning the tables. Anyway that was all right until Prentice went and produced a fine and apparently genuine alibi, which meant more trouble for Potts. So what does he do? He goes off to Jason and says that if he doesn't refute the alibi, he, Potts, will expose him as the king of the dirty-book world – we now know that from Jason himself. Jason chooses the lesser of two evils and deciding he would sooner incur Prentice's wrath rather than the execution of Potts's threat, he rats on Prentice. Then what happens?'

A small frown of annoyance crossed Mr. Gupp's brow as Manton seized on what he had intended to be another purely rhetorical question.

'Prentice disappears again, sir. He threatens Potts and then curses Jason down the phone. In the course of one of these calls when the hunt for him is on, Jason tells him that everything can be satisfactorily explained and suggests they should meet secretly by the well, a lonely rendezvous both of them are well acquainted with – I should say, sir, that Jason won't of course admit all this in so many words, but I'm quite satisfied it's what happened. Jason now saw the opportunity of ridding himself of two increasingly troublesome clients, Potts and Prentice. He never, of course, had any intention of meeting Prentice by the well and on the contrary armed himself with a one hundred per cent unbreakable alibi for that night, which embraced his daughter as well. He next led Potts to believe that Prentice was after him – for by this time Jason can have had no doubt that Potts was a murderer – and he succeeded in thoroughly putting the wind up him. A casual mention that Prentice would be standing beside a lonely well at a certain hour on a dark night was as good as handing Potts the warrant for Prentice's execution.'

'Diabolical', Mr. Gupp said.

'Afterwards of course it was in Pott's interest for the body to remain undiscovered for as long as possible. Jason's, however, required that it should be found promptly if his alibi was to be effective. Accordingly, he sent us that anonymous letter directing our attention to the well.'

There followed a ruminative silence, broken by Mr. Dalrymple who, turning a page of his brief, said:

'I suppose Mrs. Potts's evidence at the preliminary hearing was all lies.'

Mr. Otter nodded sadly.

'The usual case of a wife committing perjury to save her husband', he said.

Mr. Dalrymple demurred.

'I should have thought it was done much more to bolster her own self-esteem and salvage what she could from the wreckage. Notley was dead and the humiliating truth about their relationship would not only harm her husband but damn herself. I don't doubt that the defending solicitors were quick to point that out to her when she made contact with them after she had read of her husband's arrest.'

'Yes', Manton said. 'Incidentally she was staying in a small Kensington hotel under an assumed name. We haven't been able to get a written statement from her but she's explained one matter that bothered me. On the evening of Notley's death, she tried unsuccessfully to phone him and when she left her music meeting she walked home via his flat. He wasn't in, of course, since it was about the time he was being burnt to death in his garage, and that, not unnaturally perhaps, scared her into lying later about her movements that evening. She wanted to see him because she was desperately worried about the attempt on Prentice's life and the extent to which she might at any moment find herself involved. She wished to discover how much he proposed to say about things if he were suddenly arrested and charged with attempted murder.'

Mr. Gupp placed the tips of his fingers together and assumed a portentous air.

'This young fellow Trevane,' he said, 'he's been a bit of a young ass too, hasn't he? First of all he gets involved giving evidence in a dirty-book case and then because he's jealous of Claudia Jason going out with Notley he hangs about the hotel where they're dining and afterwards is too frightened to come forward and tell the truth.'

'Y-yes,' Manton said slowly, 'though I think that for a short time Claudia even thought it was he who'd killed Notley. After all there he was, the jealous sweetheart and a witness of their row, a row in which Notley laid hands on her – and very soon after Notley is dead.'

Playford turned to Manton.

'Remember that bit of conversation we overheard in Jason's office, "The police must never find out". I told you it would turn out to be relevant. Obviously it referred to Trevane's presence in the vicinity at the time of the murder.'

Mr. Gupp massaged the top of his nose and cleared his throat to call the meeting to order.

'I think it's worth calling Trevane's additional evidence at the trial', he said.

'You mean, sir, about his identifying Potts's voice in court as the person who phoned him in connection with the hiring of the car?'

'Yes.'

'That was an unforseeable triumph for our newly installed loudspeaker system', Playford said dryly. 'We never dreamt it would assist in identifying murderers.'

'It seems he half recognized Potts's voice when he sat in court one day a week or so ago', Manton added. 'He knew something had struck a vague chord in his memory, but he couldn't pin it down.'

The consultation was reaching the final stage of desultroy comments and questions.

'It must have been a tricky job fixing that explosive in the car', Mr. Dalrymple remarked with a yawn.

Manton smiled.

'Potts gave himself partially away over that, though I didn't notice it. When he was establishing his alibi, he quite gratuitously described how he'd repaired his radio set. That should have been a nudge in the ribs but it wasn't: not many people are sufficiently knowledgeable about electrical circuits and the like to mend their own sets. Trouble was that at that time I was too busily chasing another hare, namely the fact that Notley had served with the Royal Engineers, and I completely missed the other scent.'

Mr. Gupp leant forward and said earnestly:

'I know it has nothing to do with the presentation of this case, but what goes hard with me is the way this arch-villain Jason gets away with everything. Has any consideration been given to drawing the Law Society's attention to his activities? It's quite scandalous that he should be able to continue preying on the public. His whole conduct reeks of infamy.'

'Inspector Playford and I have had a long chat with him since Potts was committed for trial,' Manton said with a guileless expression, 'and he has told us of his intention to retire from practice and leave the district.'

'I didn't know that', Mr. Otter said in surprise.

'It's quite a recent decision, sir', Manton replied.

'Is his daughter going to run the practice on her own then?'

'No; I understand that she intends to forsake the law for marriage and settle down as Mrs. Trevane. The practice will be sold – *goodwill* and all.'

'There is one final point', Mr. Gupp said peering over the top of his spectacles. 'What was the object of all those questions about that book *Curly Christine and the Monk* or whatever it was called?'

'The questions were designed to show Jason's complicity in the obscene-book racket, but they're rather boomeranged. You see, a consignment of that particular book – it was a newly-arrived batch – was in Jason's house for only one hour before being stored away in the cache and Potts must have seen it through a window during that short period.'

'I still don't understand', Mr. Gupp said.

'That book was in Jason's house only between eight-thirty when Prentice unpacked the new consignment and just after half past nine when he stored them in the cache on his way to his nine-forty-five appointment with Notley – an appointment he never kept because the fire alarm went before he ever had time to get near the garage. In fact, after hiding the books by the well, he returned straight to Jason's house.'

Mr. Gupp's jaw dropped.

'So-o, it's yet further proof Potts was not at home all that evening. But what was he doing skulking round Jason's place?'

'Most likely he intended visiting him on his way to see Notley but changed his mind when he chanced to see the two of them poring over dirty books as he approached the house. If so, it was not only a momentous incident but a momentous alteration of plan which had the profoundest effect on everything that followed.'

Carefully tying his brief with its piece of white tape, Mr. Gupp said:

'Indeed, yes.' Then he added, 'If Jason is wise, he'll retire beyond these shores with the minimum of delay.'

Manton appeared to study the floor between his knees. Without looking up he said:

'I rather gather that the invitations to his house-warming party have already been issued and that it coincides with the opening of Wenley Assizes.'

'Oh, where?' asked Mr. Gupp in surprise as all eyes were suddenly turned avidly on Manton.

'Cuba. It seems that with considerable foresight he built a house there several years ago.' With a wry smile he added, 'And has appropriately named it JASON'S FLEECE.'

›› If you've enjoyed this book and would like to discover more great vintage crime and thriller titles, as well as the most exciting crime and thriller authors writing today, visit: ››

The Murder Room
Where Criminal Minds Meet

themurderroom.com

www.ingramcontent.com/pod-product-compliance
Ingram Content Group UK Ltd.
Pitfield, Milton Keynes, MK11 3LW, UK
UKHW040436280225
455666UK00003B/117